NIGHT OF THE LIVING ZED

Also by Basil Sylvester
The Fabulous Zed Watson!

Also by Kevin Sylvester
Apartment 713
The Fabulous Zed Watson!
MiNRS trilogy
The Almost Epic Squad: Mucus Mayhem
The Neil Flambé Capers
The Hockey Super Six series

NIGHT
OF THE
LIVING ZED

BASIL SYLVESTER AND KEVIN SYLVESTER

HarperCollins*Publishers*Ltd

Published by HarperCollins Publishers Ltd

First edition

HarperCollins Publishers Ltd
Bay Adelaide Centre, East Tower
22 Adelaide Street West, 41st Floor
Toronto, Ontario, Canada
M5H 4E3

www.harpercollins.ca

Library and Archives Canada Cataloguing in Publication

Title: Night of the living Zed / Basil Sylvester and Kevin Sylvester.
Names: Sylvester, Basil, author. | Sylvester, Kevin, author.
Identifiers: Canadiana (print) 20230528333 | Canadiana (ebook) 20230528341 |
ISBN 9781443469203 (hardcover) | ISBN 9781443469210 (ebook)
Subjects: LCGFT: Novels.
Classification: LCC PS8637.Y4175 N54 2024 | DDC jC813/.6—dc23

Printed and bound in the United States
23 24 25 26 27 LBC 5 4 3 2 1

To Erin and David, who gave me a serious case of wedding-on-the-brain while I was writing this book.
—B.S.

To all the people who don't ban books . . .
—K.S.

NIGHT OF THE LIVING ZED

MIND OF THE WORLD

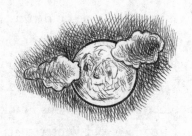

CHAPTER I

TRICKS AND TREATS

The sun was setting. An eerie cool mist settled around the nearby houses. The house I stood before was barely visible in the gathering gloom. I shivered.

I walked up the rickety front stairs, paused for a second, then rang the doorbell.

"Mrs. Gianelli? Are you there?"

I waited, holding my breath. No answer. I frowned. Then I rang the doorbell again. A cat hissed in the distance. Still no answer.

I turned to my green-hued companion and spoke clearly, despite my long sharp fangs. "You give it a try."

My companion, my best friend Gabe, shook his head. "Um . . . I can't really lift my arms in this costume."

"I know this is your first time doing this, but don't call it a costume. You need to be *one* with your monster."

"That'd be easier if I could move without making my head slide off." To demonstrate, Gabe lifted a hand, forcing up the right shoulder of his enormous Frankenstein's monster suit—one of my dad's old winter coats. The shoulder bumped his big green head (a hockey helmet with a wig glued on top) and knocked it askew.

I nudged the head back in place.

"*Boooooooooo*-m!" I said, mimicking an explosion.

"Boooooooo-m?"

"That's what an exploding ghost sounds like."

Gabe blinked. "Meaning?"

"Meaning your costume conundrum just blew up the spooky vibe we were nurturing."

Gabe rolled his eyes. "It's barely dark out yet. She might not even be home."

I shook my head. "Oh, she's home. I'm taking points off for punctuality."

Gabe still didn't make a move to ring the bell.

"Fine. I guess this is a job for Count Dracula," I said with my best classic Dracula impression—Bela Lugosi, to be precise (which, if I'm being honest, is impeccable). I pushed the button again and counted to ten, this time with my best Count von Count voice—also, TBH, top-notch. "One-ah-ah-ah, Two-ah-ah-ah . . ."

Finally, the door slowly opened a crack, and Mrs. Gianelli's face appeared in the sliver of light. She was wearing an apron and holding a large knife!

"AHHHH!" Gabe screamed.

I reached out and grabbed his arm to stop him from bolting. "Trick or treat!" I said.

"It's October 9." Mrs. Gianelli closed the door slightly.

"Yup. Halloween-O-ween." I beamed.

"Halloween-O-ween . . . already?" She lowered the knife.

Gabe relaxed, so I let him go. I held up my tombstone-shaped clipboard and clicked my bone-shaped pen. "Time for our annual pre-Halloween inspection."

"I'm just making din—"

"I admit it's a little earlier than last year. Didn't you get my flyer with the date change?"

She sighed and rolled her eyes.

Some adults, I have found, do not appreciate the preparation involved in setting up the perfect Halloween.

Oh sure, they'll happily decorate a dead pine tree weeks before Christmas. They'll even brag about getting their shopping done months ahead of time. But ask them to put just a little prep into the *only* holiday that lets you be whatever you want to be? With all the theatricality, the candy, the PURE JOY? What Gabe calls the *ne plus ultra* and I call the super-duper-stupendousest of all holidays?

Well, getting adults to prep for *that* is like pulling fangs.

3

"Gabe and I are just triple-checking that everyone is getting things ready."

"Are they serious?" She raised an eyebrow at Gabe.

I smiled to myself and added a checkmark to her score sheet. Points deducted for punctuality, but points gained for the right pronouns. Thanks, Mrs. G!

"Yeah, they're serious." Gabe shrugged, loosening the helmet again. "Happy Halloween-O-ween?"

She turned back to me. "Okay, Zed, fire away."

A few questions later, we turned and left. "Another successful Halloween-O-ween check." I consulted my tombstone clipboard. "Mrs. Gianelli agreed to upgrade from licorice sticks—seriously!—to candy bars."

"She was already planning to decorate her porch," said Gabe.

"With just two pumpkins and a scarecrow!" I said. "But now she's going to add spooky lights and maybe even some fog. This earns her house a four-out-of-five pumpkin rating on our official Halloween map."

"Is your mom still going to print them off at work?"

I nodded. "Then we can hand them out to all the little trick-or-treating ghouls. Now who's next?" I ran my finger down our list. "Aha!" I pointed to the end of the street.

"Mr. Ohi. Last year, he handed out bags of candy corn, if you can believe that."

"I remember," Gabe said. "I actually don't mind candy corn."

"Ugh. It's an automatic one-pumpkin rating!"

"So is Halloween-O-ween about improving our personal candy haul?"

"We are doing it for the *children*, Gabe. We need our neighborhood to keep its reputation as the best and scariest in the city."

"Kids do come from all over to trick-or-treat here," Gabe said with a small smile. (Anything more enthusiastic would have knocked his head off again.) "They even asked about it in that interview we did for the radio."

"Exactly. Which we get to hear tomorrow morning!"

"If we can get up that early."

"I've set six alarms in different rooms."

"But you're sleeping over at my house. You set alarms at *my* house?"

"Of course. You and your family hold on to old electronics until they're fire hazards."

"My dad likes old tech."

"So old the snooze buttons don't work, so you *have* to wake up when they go off," I said, rubbing my hands together.

5

Gabe rolled his eyes so hard, his forehead slid a little more.

I nudged it back in place and tightened the strap that held it under his chin. "The other advantage of Halloween-O-ween is that we can practice walking and ringing doorbells in our frightening finery."

"Like a dress rehearsal."

"Maybe for a Halloween-y opera," I said. Gabe had taken me to a few operas, and while they weren't as boring as I thought they'd be, nothing has ever been made worse with a little Halloween spice.

Gabe smiled. "Have you ever seen the headpieces from *Aida*?"

"No, but do tell." I didn't always get the music part, but the opera costumes? Frequent winners of the Zed seal of approval.

"Ornate! Like, you can always spot her, Princess Aida, when she marches onto the stage, even before she starts singing."

"Warns the audience it's time to put in the earplugs." I grinned.

"Haha."

"Enough of opera. Time to complete the pre-Halloween haunting of our neighborhood haunts!"

The moon was smiling down on us as we secured more promises to step up the confections and decorations.

"We have done spooktacular work, Frankie," I said, patting Gabe on the back. "With each strobe light, spooky fog machine and full-size chocolate bar, the children of this city will thank us."

Gabe finally took off his helmet. "That's better," he sighed. "Dinner's probably ready."

"Your dad's lasagna?" My stomach rumbled. "With his secret ingredients?"

"Yup. My homegrown basil and oregano." Gabe smiled, which was nice. He and his dad didn't always see eye to eye, but our success in our first literary adventure (ever heard of *The Monster's Castle*?) had led to some progress. Old Man Linden still didn't get Gabe's aversion to sports and love of Latin, but he was coming around on the opera and plant stuff.

I meditatively chewed a Snickers—a leftover from my Zed-approved Halloween-O-ween sample handout package—as we made our way to Gabe's house.

"This Halloween is going to be the best ever," I said, dancing around Gabe and waving a hand like a fluttering bat around his head. "Wooooooh, so spooooooky!" I encouraged him to join in my celebratory Halloween serenade.

Gabe shuddered slightly. I cut it out; I'd forgotten he wasn't the biggest fan of bats and ghosts.

We turned the corner onto Gabe's street and saw a familiar pile of junk appearing through the mist.

"CARSSANDRA?!"

Yes! The 1996 Subaru Impreza that helped us solve the mystery of a lifetime— sometimes with working A/C— had appeared unexpectedly like a phantom chariot.

Gabe and I ran over and hugged the parked car (which wasn't easy in our getups), then burst through the front door of Gabe's house.

Sure enough, Sam, Gabe's sister and the owner of Carssandra (formerly known as Dolly CARton), and her awesome girlfriend, Jo, were setting out plates on the dining room table. They turned as we bolted into the room.

"Hey, look, it's the dynamic doofuses!" said Sam, wrapping Gabe in her arms.

"We didn't know you two were in town!" I said, hugging Jo.

They exchanged a glance, and my Extra Zed-sory Perception (or EZP, for short) started tingling.

"It's a bit of a surprise visit," Jo said. She was definitely giving off "we've got news" vibes.

Sam nodded. "We've got news."

CHAPTER 2

LET THE BELLS RING OUT

I sat as still as I could, trembling with anticipation, waiting for the telltale creak on the topmost step.

CREAK!

"Okay, Gabe—hit it!"

Gabe, sitting on the piano stool next to me, started tickling the ivories, and I belted out in my loudest voice, "Here come the briiiiiiides! All dressed in . . . *pajamas*?!"

Sam and Jo appeared at the top of the stairs in some truly boring gray-checked flannels. I forced myself to look away, made a mental note to give them some fashion advice before they walked down the aisle and ended the song with ". . . sweet love united for GE-O-LOGY!!!!"

Gabe finished the march with a flourish.

"That rocked!" I high-fived Gabe.

Sam and Jo reached the bottom stair, glowered at us, then slunk into the kitchen.

"I think they liked it," I said.

"It's a great song. The original is from the Wagner opera *Lohengrin.* Completely different words in German. It's for the wedding scene in act—"

"Yeah, yeah. Cool, cool." I waved my hand at Gabe and quickly followed my favorite couple through the door and into the kitchen. They were sitting at the table, staring down at the breakfast Gabe's dad had made before hitting the shower.

Sam and Jo had told us about their engagement the night before, but then we'd had dinner, and who can speak more than a few words when world-class lasagna is on the table? Then they'd rushed out to tell their friends the news and came back late. I had questions, and luckily, two of the alarms I'd set had been on the clocks in their room.

"Good morning, lovebirds!" I called. "I can't believe you're getting MARRIED!" I mimed firing Cupid's arrow at them.

Their response was something between a growl and a louder growl.

Sam spotted the decorations I'd added to their bowls of

oatmeal. Smiley faces made out of M&M's, blueberries and squeezable icing. I'd even used the spoons to make it look like the bowls had arms.

Jo arched an eyebrow. "Why are they punching each other?"

"They're holding hands!" I said. "Like the brides on a wedding cake. And it'll taste as good as it looks."

"That's what I'm afraid of," Sam said.

"Hmph. Great artists are never appreciated in their time."

Gabe walked in. "So did I miss any of the wedding plans?"

"YES!" I slammed my hands on the table. Sam and Jo jumped in their seats. "We must have details! Date? Venue? What are you going to wear? Please don't say gray flannels. Flowers? Pets? Music choice: DJ or live band? Please no opera."

Gabe looked hurt.

"Okay, fine," I said. "But only Italian opera."

Gabe smiled, and I resumed my interrogation.

"Menu? Venue? Rings? Ring bearers? I accept, BTW. I can also double as a flower kid or usher. WHAT KIND OF CAKE?????!!!!!!"

"Whoa, whoa, Zed," Sam said, rubbing her temples. "I got up a little earlier than I expected to."

"You're welcome."

She started to get out of her chair. "*You* set that alarm?"

"Both of them, actually, including the one I hid in your closet. Always have a backup."

Sam's arm muscles flexed. My eyes darted to the butter knife on the table.

"It's okay, right, Sam?" said Jo, putting a hand on her shoulder. "We were getting up early anyway. And, Zed, we haven't had our third cups of coffee yet. Let's all take a deep breath."

Sam sat back down. "We're keeping it small," she said through clenched teeth.

"Oh, so you're saying the reception might have to be on a yacht instead of a cruise ship? We can roll with that."

Jo snorted. "Just family and a few friends. Leslie will come up and—"

"ALOYSIUS WILL BE SO EXCITED!!!!" I jumped up and down. Aloysius is my stuffed jackalope. He was made by Leslie, Jo's uncle.

Sam wagged her finger. "No jackalopes."

"But I'm dressing him up in a pumpkin costume! He's a jack-a-lope-a-lantern!"

"N-O."

"You fiend."

"The guest list is very limited," Jo said.

"Very." Sam glared at me over her coffee. "And getting more limited by the second."

"It's okay"—I turned to Gabe—"you can be my plus-one." He snorted.

Sam actually spat out some coffee, then shrieked as more gushed out her nose. Jo grabbed a napkin and dabbed her chin. It was so cute I had to rush over and hug them.

"OUCH! MY RIBS!" said Sam.

I released them.

Gabe sipped his freshly squeezed orange juice. "Back to the wedding. How do you actually define 'small'?"

Jo picked a few blueberries from her oatmeal. "As small as possible. Weddings are expensive, and we're students, so we don't have much cash. And we want to have the ceremony soon, while we're both up here working on our PhD theses. So we want to keep the planning simple too."

Sam croaked, "We also want to help pay for Leslie and Jennie to come up."

"Jennie!!!" Gabe and I shrieked.

Jo smiled. "She's taking a weekend off so her diner can get a fresh coat of paint. She offered to do the catering!"

Jennie's diner was one of the coolest places I'd ever been. Gabe and I still drooled at the memory of the amazing fry bread she'd made for us.

"OOHH! Has she cooked for a couple of hundred people before?"

Sam sighed. "Small wedding, Zed. S-M-A-L-L. Like your ability to listen."

"We want a simple ceremony," Jo added. "A few guests. That's it."

I snorted. Lots of my relatives had gotten married, and every one of them had said "We want a simple wedding." But what they really meant was "We can't afford the wedding we want."

Everyone wants a big romantic night filled with family, friends and people you barely know dancing in a gilded hall as they toss confetti in the air and stay up way too late. But as Jo said, weddings are *not* cheap.

"But if you could, you'd go crazy, right? Cake the size of the Monster's Castle? Matching purple-and-green linen jumpsuits? White roses on every table? Stretch limo? Maybe a Halloween theme?!"

"We *like* simple, Zed," Jo and Sam said together. It sounded like they'd rehearsed it to convince themselves.

"Riiiight," I said, winking at Gabe. He winked back, which meant our minds were now clicking. Which is how we start hatching plans.

"Why are you two winking?" Sam pointed a finger at us. Darn, she was good.

I pretended to wipe away a tear. "We're just so happy for you both."

"Don't cook up some cockamamie plan, you two."

I was about to salute her use of the word "cockamamie" when Gabe's dad rushed into the kitchen, his hair still wet.

"Turn on the radio!"

"Why?"

"The interview has started!"

My eyes locked on the kitchen clock. We'd been so swept up in the wedding interrogation that we'd missed the start of the show!

Gabe leapt up and switched on the ancient brown radio on the counter. It took a few seconds for the tubes to warm up (I'm not kidding), and then the interviewer's voice emerged from the static like a ghost at a seance.

"*So has the Mystery of the Monster's Castle led to more detective work?*"

A strange voice burst out of the speakers.

"*Not at the level we'd hoped. We helped find some lost library books—they were under a bench in the park. That sort of thing, so far.*"

"Who is that?" I asked.

"That's you," said Sam.

"I don't sound like that!"

"True," Sam said, smirking. "You usually sound worse."

Gabe's dad—a real estate agent who did his own radio ads—shushed us. "People always think they sound weird when they hear themselves back. Now listen."

"And how do you get new cases?"

"Word of mouth," Radio Gabe said. *"But we're always open to any kind of mystery."*

"Especially if it has ghosts and monsters," Radio Me said.

"And opera." You can guess who said that.

The interviewer laughed. *"That seems like a million-in-one chance!"*

"And if possible, ice cream."

He laughed harder. *"Well, you intrepid investigators have a great Halloween this year. I hear your neighborhood is always the one to visit."*

"We make sure of it," I said.

Then we said goodbye, and they played the theme from the TV show *The Munsters*. A+ choice.

Gabe and I got up from the kitchen table and started dancing. Jo and Sam had apparently now had their third coffees because they joined us!

Gabe's dad gave him a big hug. "My son, the radio celebrity!"

The song ended, and I bent over to catch my breath. Gabe's dad reached up to turn off the radio, then stopped.

Why?

Because the interviewer said these magic words:

"*Zed and Gabe, if you're listening . . . you are* not *going to believe the call we just got!*"

CHAPTER 3

THE MYSTERY OF GLYNDEBOURNE MANOR

An anonymous caller had phoned in to the radio show with the Mystery of Glyndebourne Manor.

Turns out, there was *a real actual haunted house*, once owned by a rich and famous artist! The caller told us to check out the website for the house. It had very little information and only one or two blurry old photos, but it did say that every twenty-five years, the manor held an epic contest. Anyone who could spend three days and two nights there without getting so scared they peed their pants and ran away screaming would be rewarded beyond their wildest dreams.

Okay, that's maybe not *exactly* what it said on the website.

More good news: it was close! Only a few hours away by car (or seventeen hundred hours in Carssandra). It had almost everything we were looking for—ghosts, mystery, even art and opera for Gabe. Ice cream wasn't mentioned on the website, but I was sure we would be able to sniff some out sooner or later.

At the bottom of the web page, there was an "Apply Here" button for the contest. I smacked that button so fast I almost broke my finger. Then I refreshed and applied again for good measure.

After my fiftieth application, Gabe had had enough.

"Zed, take a break. You're going to destroy my keyboard."

I sighed and flopped down on his bed. He sat down at his computer and clicked through the site. After a second, he exclaimed, "Oh, wow!"

I sat bolt upright. "We got in???!!!!"

"No, not yet."

I frowned, then said in my Dracula voice, "Then why are you disturbing my eternal slumber?"

"You said there was opera," said Gabe, "but you didn't say there was so much! The owner was a famous *opera costume and set designer!!!* Her name was Charlotte Scherrer. I've never heard of her, but I gotta check out her stuff. This is SO cool! I wonder if the caller was an opera fan like me."

"Mysterious caller, mysterious manor, why there's more than one opera superfan in the world—a lot of mysteries here."

Gabe chuckled.

Sam appeared in the doorway, holding up her phone. "Hey, dingbats. Why did I just get five hundred emails telling me about a haunted house contest?"

"DID WE GET IN?" I yelled.

She narrowed her eyes. "So it *was* you. Why, exactly?"

"Because Gabe won't let me use his address after the Zombie Cat Fiasco," I said.

Gabe nodded. "They tried to order—"

Sam cut him off. "I don't want to know."

I sprang to the door and grabbed her phone, breathlessly tapping on the message.

We were in! Two tickets to the contest, starting October 29.

Sam took her phone back. "I'll forward the email to Gabe. I've got stuff to do. With *my* phone. And *my* email."

"You look tired. I guess geology research is *hard* work." Hee-hee.

She rolled her eyes.

"Sam, what are you doing on October 29?" I asked.

"Let me guess. I'm going to be in Carssandra, driving you to a remote and creepy location."

Gabe and I put on our best "please, please, please" faces.

Sam sighed. "And to think I imagined coming home would be a nice break." She walked away.

I turned back to Gabe, bouncing. To my surprise, he did *not* seem excited.

"What's wrong?"

He looked up from his computer. "Just reading the email Sam forwarded. It says there are *real* ghosts there."

"I sure hope so!" I said.

I sat down on the bed next to him, and we looked at the email together. One part in the first paragraph stuck out immediately: "Charlotte's fortune is thought to be hidden within the house. Contestants will have the opportunity to discover her secrets for themselves."

"A vast fortune!" I jumped up immediately. "Okay, now we *really* have to go. I know ghosts are scary, but if there's money—"

"We could get Sam and Jo their dream wedding!" said Gabe.

I turned back to him. "Exactly!"

I began pacing the room. Charlotte's fortune would give Sam and Jo the wedding of their dreams. Yes, they kept insisting they wanted a wedding that was small and inexpensive, but Gabe and I knew that we had to get that money so they could stop kidding themselves and see that we were right.

Or they could use the money to go on a cool honeymoon! They said they didn't have time for one, but I would put my sock-and-sandaled foot down on this point. Even if they wouldn't compromise on the yacht, live band and eight-tiered wedding cake, they *had* to have a honeymoon.

"Gabe, I know you're afraid of ghosts, but sometimes you have to make sacrifices. It's for a good cause."

He stopped reading and looked up at me. "I don't know, Zed. It must be really scary if no one has been able to stay even two nights. Are we sure about this?"

I sat back down. "Gabe . . . I think it's time for an encore."

He sighed. "Really? You're 'encore'-ing me?"

I nodded. "You encored me for that *Rigoletto* opera last month."

"And you liked it! Plus, you encored me for that K-bop concert last winter."

"I said it bops. But it's not K-*bop*—it's K-pop. As in pop music. Also, what I'm hearing is that it's my turn."

"So you're using encore—our pinky-promise-no-take-backsies-you-gotta-agree code—not to go to a fun concert or a show, but to bring me to a terrifying haunted house filled with ghosts?"

"Yep. *And* you can have two freebie encores on me."

Gabe considered. "Okay," he said. "Encore."

"That's the spirit," I said.

"But there's something else," he said, pointing at his laptop screen.

"I will protect you from any supernatural forces, I promise," I said.

"No, it's not that."

"And any natural forces. You can count on me."

"Zed."

"No sacrifice is too great to give Sam and Jo their dream wedding."

"Look at these dates," he finally said. "We're going to miss Halloween."

I jumped. "Are you sure? But . . . "

Gabe and I looked at each other for a second, not saying anything. He knew my weak spot. I sighed a deep sigh and closed my eyes, picturing Sam and Jo in ugly gray pajamas, getting married in a classroom with only rocks as witnesses. I shuddered.

"Encore?" Gabe said.

Finally, I nodded. "Encore," I said with a sniffle.

CHAPTER 4

EN-CAR

October 29 arrived. Gabe, Jo, Sam and I were packed into Carssandra. Well, and Aloysius too, but he would be there just for the car trip, not for the haunted house.

"Ew, you actually brought that thing?" Sam made a face.

I ignored her and turned to Gabe. "It's been twenty minutes. Read the email from the manor again. And in your best tour guide voice!"

Sam groaned. "For real? If I have to listen to this one more time . . ."

I looked at the dashboard clock. "If we don't step on it, we'll listen to it at least five more times, actually."

Sam gunned the engine and merged into the far-left lane.

Gabe cleared his throat and spoke in a dry nasally voice, as if he were narrating a nature documentary. "Every twenty-five years, the doors to the magnificent Glyndebourne Manor open. A terrifying haunted house built by the world-famous

Charlotte Scherrer, opera set designer and costumier. The inspiration for the outside structure is the famous—"

"Get to the good part!" I urged.

"This *is* the good part," said Gabe in his normal voice. He gave a slight cough and continued his narration. "—is the famous La Scala opera house in Milan, Italy. But while the facade is a beautiful homage to the Italian monument, inside lurks some of the most terrifying paranormal activity ever seen."

"YES!" I pumped my fist in the air.

"Orientation begins at sundown on October 29, and the contest runs from the stroke of midnight on October 30 to the stroke of midnight November 1."

"So we don't technically have to miss Halloween if we can solve it faster," I said. "Then we can leave early on Halloween morning and get back in time for trick-or-treating!"

Sam snorted from the front seat. "I thought no one has ever been able to solve this—and you two think you're gonna beat the whole contest before anyone else? As if. And why do you care so much about Halloween, anyway? You're going to see real ghosts!"

Gabe shivered. "I thought you said there was no such thing as real ghosts?"

Sam banged her head on the steering wheel. "There ARE no real ghosts! I was humoring them."

"But how do you know?" said Gabe.

"THERE ARE NO GHOSTS!!!!" Sam was starting to lose it.

Jo sighed. She turned around in her seat so only I could see her face. "Zed, I appreciate your enthusiasm, but there's *definitely* not a house filled with ghosts—right?" She made a slashing motion across her neck, the universal sign for *Cut it out*. I winked back and mouthed, *Gotcha*.

"Sam and Jo are right, Gabe, there's not a house filled with a bunch of ghosts," I said, and then paused. "There's probably just one ghost."

He whimpered. Jo gave me a disapproving look.

"I agree you'll make Halloween, Zed," she said.

I perked up. "Really?"

She nodded. "You'll run out of the house tonight like a couple of scared doofuses. I say you last twenty minutes."

"Ha! That won't happen. Nothing scares the unZed."

Gabe went back to reading the email. "You don't understand, Sam. It says here that there are vintage opera props and costumes galore!"

Sam groaned. "Great, Zed, so you've lured my brother in with the promise of opera, only to scare the pants off him."

"Are you kidding me?" I gestured to his pants, which

26

were, as always, covered in pockets. "His pants are the sturdiest thing about him. I bet people could hide in his pockets and survive any disaster."

I munched anxiously on chocolate pretzels, a stage-two road trip snack. Not to be confused with a stage-one snack such as a cruller, which is eaten within a few minutes of leaving the driveway.

I smoothed out the wrinkles in my skirt and rubbed my palms on my thighs, squeezing my eyes tight and willing myself not to get worked up again.

"Speaking of pants," said Gabe, "I thought you were only wearing joggers these days."

"A flowing skirt is more dramatic. For when I run away from some specter's clutches." I paused. "Or toward them."

"Yeah, but there aren't any pockets. How are you going to carry your flashlight and notepad and stuff?"

I pointed to his pockets again. "You have more than enough storage for two."

He groaned. "Fashion before function yet again?"

"Always." I smiled. "Anyway, we are now officially late. Just like old times."

"It better not be like old times," said Sam from the front seat. "My A/C hasn't busted since Jo fixed it last summer, so don't jinx it."

"I would never let your A/C break again, babe," said Jo, reaching across to squeeze Sam's shoulder.

"Our relationship is purely mercenary, I admit," said Sam, laughing. "Nothing beats having a 24/7 mechanic."

"And Carssandra really does need it," I said with a snort.

"Hey, pal! Could you BE any slower?!" Sam growled at the car in front of us.

"Why can't Jo drive us?" I said.

"Because *I* can look at the GPS without getting sick, and Samantha, for all her lovely qualities, would toss her cookies all over me, you and the entire car if she were in the passenger seat."

"Well, thank you, Jo. I feel *so* appreciated," she said.

Jo cleared her throat. "What's the communication like in the definitely-not-haunted house? Any phones allowed?"

"Nope, we're going full Edwardian era." I grabbed Gabe's sleeve and continued in a hoarse whisper, "I bet the service is really spotty, maybe even nonexistent—the perfect conditions for a haunting or a seance."

"Zed, come on. That's enough," said Jo, but Gabe was already back to geeking out about the opera stuff.

"I wonder if they'll have some of the original backdrops or stage paintings," he said. "This Charlotte person was a costume *and* set designer. I saw online a beautiful set she made for *The Magic Flute*, for the Queen of the Night's aria, all painted with these unbelievably brilliant golden stars. It's so magical."

"Speaking of magic," Sam said, "I bet this haunted house is going to be all cheap magic tricks and stuff. Not scary at all."

We got off the highway and started to drive on tiny crooked roads. The sun had completely set, and the tree branches, bare of leaves, twisted like clawed hands, beckoning us ever farther. After about fifteen minutes of navigating these roads in the twilight, Jo exclaimed while looking at her phone, "Turn right here!"

There was no real sign—just a post with a house number. Sam swore but managed the turn. Gabe pressed his nose to the window, peering into the distance to see if he could make anything out. The headlights swept across dozens of ghostly white trees. Their trunks seemed to have eyes looking back at us. Beyond that, it was pitch dark.

"The GPS says we're here?" said Jo, looking at her phone again. She pinched and zoomed in on her map, then whistled. "Oh, wait! No, this is just the *grounds*. It's still a ten-minute drive to get to the house. Whoa!"

We finally reached the gravel drive almost half an hour late. I opened the car door and got out. A shiver ran through me—but from excitement, not fear or cold. I guess I was sort of—to use one of my mom's favorite words—gobsmacked.

The house, illuminated by silvery moonlight, was *huge*, at least four stories tall, with so many pillars and arches, you couldn't even tell where the actual entrance was at first. It looked about half a city block long. In the faint light, the many arched windows seemed like mouths, ready to swallow those foolish enough to get closer.

But it was also beautiful. Everywhere I looked, there was a different material—glass, stained glass, marble, stone, a rounded red-brick turret. And in the center, rising above everything, a huge pointed roof made of thick timber.

"This place is bizarre," I heard Sam say.

"Huh," said Jo behind me. "That roof looks like a pyramid."

"A pyramid someone made from gluing together parts of at least ten different buildings," said Sam.

"It's *perfect*," I said, still staring.

"La Scala!" Gabe cheered. "It's just like being there. Sort of." He looked like a kid who had just been handed a full-size candy bar.

There was no time to waste.

I grabbed him. "Gabe, we gotta go!" I started to drag him toward the house. He waved and I called "Byethankyou!" over my shoulder, then I pulled us both up the wooden stairs to the porch.

The steps groaned underfoot as we thundered up them.

"Hey, careful! I almost tripped!" Gabe said.

"No time!" I replied, and I grabbed the huge doorknob and pushed us inside.

CHAPTER 5

DIS-ORIENTATION

At first, we couldn't see much. The foyer through the main entrance was only dimly lit by a few small lamps. There was a huge staircase directly in front of us, with a landing and then more stairs branching off to the left and the right.

We didn't have time to take it all in. A small handwritten sign taped to one of the staircase banisters said "LIBRARY➡" with an arrow pointing to the door on our right.

"That's where we go to check in," I said. "Come on!!" And before Gabe could protest, I dragged him through the door and on to our uncertain fate.

We burst into the library like we were rock stars taking to the stage. But we had no audience; the room was empty.

"Are we sure this is the right place?" Gabe asked, his words swallowed up by the air.

"That's what the email said."

"Maybe we're too late?"

"Maybe . . ." I trailed off. "Wait, do you hear that? It sounds like . . . voices."

"I don't hear anything," said Gabe, shifting from foot to foot. "This place is creepy enough without you trying to scare me more."

"I'm not! You can't hear because you're always listening to your headphones super loud and your ears are busted."

"I can hear you being a goof loud and clear."

"Haha. But I definitely heard something." I cupped my hand around my ear and stepped farther into the room. There were voices, but I couldn't tell where they were coming from. I was just puzzling this out when a section of the paneled wall to our left swung open and a short woman wearing paint-splattered overalls walked through, saying over her shoulder, "And here we are, back in the library. Again, once you've—oh!" She noticed us and jumped. "I'm sorry. You startled me."

"Are you talking to ghosts?!" I asked.

"No, I'm talking to these two." She gestured behind her, but I couldn't see anyone. "And we're closed for visitors this weekend, I'm sorry." Her voice was husky. She doffed her plaid hat to us, then put it back on. It was one of those old-timey newsboy caps that sat mostly flat on her head. I liked her immediately.

"Actually, we're here to check in! For the haunted house!" I said. "The contest!"

"Sorry we're late," added Gabe. "We had some car trouble."

She beamed at us. "Well! Glad you could join us."

"Us?" said Gabe, looking around fearfully.

"Us," she repeated. She walked forward, smiling and extending her hand in greeting.

I gave a little bow, and when I looked up again, two people had appeared behind her. One of them was a tall man wearing a plaid dress shirt over a T-shirt with a sci-fi logo. He looked at us and seemed unimpressed. I felt Gabe straighten beside me. The other, a woman, was shorter and wore a flowy floral dress and had her long hair in a tight braid.

Rats, no ghosts yet, I thought. Or at least not cool ones.

"Well, here we are!" said the woman in the newsboy cap, shaking Gabe's hand. "This is . . . no, don't tell me. I'll

34

remember! This is Dan." She pointed to the guy in the plaid shirt. "And this is Soraya, and I'm Bertie."

Soraya smiled and gave a little wave.

The man cleared his throat. "Actually, it's Dean."

But Bertie didn't seem to notice him.

"Well, I'm Zed, and this is Gabe."

"What kind of name is Zed?" I heard Dean whisper to Soraya.

I frowned but ignored him.

"And these are our permission forms," I said, reaching around to grab them from my backpack. I grabbed only air.

Then I gasped. "Gabe, our stuff! Sam and Jo still have it!"

I ran out to the porch, panting and panicked, and leapt off the steps. But I couldn't see them.

"Hey, bozo," I heard Sam's voice say in the gloom.

Two headlights cut through the dark, and I could suddenly see Sam and Jo leaning against Carssandra, holding two backpacks—one was gray and had many pockets (Gabe's, obviously), and the other was small, patent leather (well, fake leather) and in the shape of a coffin.

"You guys are still here?!" I ran over.

"You've literally been inside for all of five minutes," said Sam. "Scared away already, huh?"

"I guess I owe you five bucks," said Jo. "I thought they'd last at least twenty minutes." She looked at me.

I was too hurt to speak. "I'm too hurt to speak," I said out loud.

Jo smiled. "Nah, we're just kidding you. We realized you left your bags—plus, we didn't get a proper goodbye."

I hugged them both tight. Jo tousled my hair.

"I want to get a picture," she said. "Gabe, get over here!" She waved to Gabe, who was coming down the porch steps.

"Sorry, had to go slow," he called out. "Almost tripped on these stairs on the way in. They're kind of rotted. But that happens with older wood. They should have gone with cedar, maybe—"

"Sure, sure," said Sam. "Just get your butt next to the creature—and Aloysius too."

I almost protested this jab but decided it was actually a very good Zed-like joke. "Sam, I applaud you." I bowed before her.

She rolled her eyes.

Jo held up her instant camera. Sam stood next to her. "Okay, say 'Jackalopes are creepy' on three. One, two, three!"

The flash was so bright I saw spots for a second. I watched the photo develop, and then gasped and pointed to the upper corner.

"What *is* that?!" There was a small but noticeable wisp of *something* in one of the windows behind us.

"It looks like the flash reflecting off the glass," said Jo. She studied it again. "But who knows?"

"Can I keep this?" I asked. "It might be evidence of a ghost."

Jo considered. "How about I take it to my 'lab' and see what I can find out?"

I nodded. "Good thinking. Photo-spectral analysis."

She winked. Honestly, I think Jo wished she could join us inside.

Gabe frowned. "It's just the flash, though, right?"

Jo smiled. "A hundred percent. Nothing to worry about."

I hugged Aloysius goodbye, then slipped the seatbelt over his furry little body.

"Okay, let's get back in there," I said to Gabe, and we walked up the steps carefully.

This time, Bertie was waiting for us in the foyer. "Grabbed your stuff? All ready? Let's get you back in the library to finish up. And we have a special surprise in store."

Bertie walked in ahead of us and turned on the lights. It took me a second to notice, but then it hit me.

"Light switches? I thought this house would have gas

lamps," I said, trying to hide my disappointment. Gas lamps, I felt, would have been more suitably creepy.

"Trust me, be glad it's electric. Gas lamps are pretty dangerous—there used to be a lot of fires and explosions in old houses like this. Back in the day, electricity was kind of an expensive novelty, actually. Very new and cool at the time. Now, of course, the wiring in this house is so old that the lights aren't that bright and outages are frequent, so it's still pretty scary, even for me."

"Fire hazards and old electronics? A home away from home," joked Gabe.

Now that we were back in the library, I made sure to take in my surroundings properly. The email had said we had to solve a mystery while being chased by ghosts. Anything could be a clue.

The room was big, almost the length of a school gym, but much narrower, maybe about twenty paces across. I couldn't believe how much I'd missed when we first entered. Everything was paneled with dark wood (I made a mental note to ask Gabe the plant expert what kind of wood it was). There were clusters of comfy-looking armchairs at either end of the room, and almost the entire floor was covered in a deep, soft rug decorated with flowers and birds.

To our right, against the wall behind the chairs, were several glass display cabinets.

"What are those?" I asked.

Bertie looked where I was pointing. There were five tall

cases with ornate costumes inside and a handful of smaller cases filled with other sparkly stuff.

"Those are some of Charlotte's most famous—and some say, best—work," Bertie explained.

Gabe gasped. "Are those the . . . *originals?*" He spoke in a whisper.

Bertie nodded. "Oh yeah."

He clapped a hand over his mouth, too awestruck to speak. They were definitely more Gabe's thing than mine, but one costume did catch my eye: it was bright green and covered in what looked like dragon scales.

Across from the doorway there were three large paned windows arching like mouths, just like the windows we had seen from the driveway at the front of the house. I did a quick memory scan of how we had entered the building and decided that these windows faced west. Under them was a small carved wooden table with a few wooden chairs ranged around it.

I looked left, in the direction of the secret door that Bertie and the other two had come through. How had I missed the *huge* portrait hanging over a mantelpiece at the far end of the room?

It was large but, like the library itself, narrow. The painting was a full-body portrait of a woman who I took to be Charlotte. She stood against a simple gray background. Unlike her flamboyant house and costumes, she was dressed simply in a black gown with a high collar and long sleeves.

She wore no jewelry other than a small plain necklace, and she had her hands folded in front of her. She looked straight out at the viewer—not smiling, but not frowning either. She had a sort of sadness about her.

Bertie flicked on another set of lights, and suddenly, the frame around the painting glowed like it was made of gold.

Bertie noticed me looking. "That's Charlotte. She's beautiful, isn't she?"

"She is," I said.

Next to me, Gabe gasped, "And that frame! So cool!"

Bertie nodded. "Specific kind of reflective paint, hit at just the right angle with spotlighting. Used in a lot of theaters during that era to really make the space feel 'alive and luminous with light,' in Charlotte's description. She was a master at that kind of effect."

I cocked my head. "But why is she dressed like that? Look at her house so far—it's much more over the top."

"Well, black is typically used for mourning clothes," said Bertie. "But I don't know if she was mourning, and if so, for whom. She never married or had children. Maybe she put all her creative energy into her work and not her outfits?"

"Couldn't be me," I said.

Gabe smiled and pointed to my coffin backpack. "Duh."

"So now that we're all here, I'll repeat the ground rules," Bertie said, gesturing for us to sit in the huge armchairs at both ends of the room. "Dan and Soraya, entertain yourselves, as you've already heard this."

Dean yawned and lazily began examining the books.

"I don't mind hearing it all again," said Soraya, sitting in a chair close to us and resting her chin on her hands.

"Suit yourself," said Bertie. "Okay, so after we wrap up here—I'll explain in a second, Zed—I'll escort you to your rooms. You'll have read this in the email, but the contest officially starts at midnight. This evening is for orientation, as well as getting comfortable and rested for the challenges ahead."

Soraya gave an excited squeak. "This is where the ghosts come in," she said.

Bertie put up a hand to stop her. "The ghosts don't work on any schedule, Soraya. After you wake up, *if* you wake up"— she winked—"you will begin moving through the house. When the clock strikes midnight on All Saints' Day—that's November 1—you'll be escorted off the property."

"Where do we get escorted to?" asked Gabe.

Bertie paused. "That's a good question. I don't really know. No one's ever made it that far. I guess I'll bring you out to the parking lot? Bottom line, you have until 11:59 on Halloween night to make it all the way through the manor."

Soraya gave another excited squeak. "Oh, that's right! *This* is where the ghosts come in."

Bertie gave a weary smile. "The rules are simple. You can move around from room to room, but you can't exit through the same door you came in. If you do, you forfeit."

"But if we can't leave from the door we entered, where are we supposed to go?" I asked.

"You'll see," said Bertie, then she paused and knit her eyebrows together. "Oh, you know what? Darn it, I forgot something. I'll go get it. Mingle and so on until I'm back." And with a wave of her arm in the general direction of Dean, she hurried out. The door to the library didn't even make a sound as it closed.

Well, as you may already know, when Zed Watson is told to mingle, they mingle. In fact, even when they are not told to, they will. It's simply in my (super)nature. I turned

to Gabe to ask him what he wanted to do, but he was back standing in front of one of the cases.

"Zed, look! It's the headpiece I was telling you about!" His nose was almost squished against the case. When I walked over to where he was standing, his breath was fogging up the glass. "The one from *Aida*!" he said, pointing.

Without waiting for me to answer, he moved to another case, oohing and ahhing. He stood in front of one holding a huge fur cloak trimmed with what looked like gold thread. It seemed cool, but since there weren't any ghosts around that I could see, I decided to chat with some real live humans. I walked over to Dean and Soraya.

"Well, howdy!" I waved at them. Dean did a weary half nod. "Are you really the only other two people who showed up? How did you find out about it? Do you like ghosts? Are you paranormal investigators?"

They seemed to be having trouble keeping up. My mom's words came floating back to me: "Slow down when talking to adults, Zed. They aren't as clever or attentive as children."

I took a breath and started again. "So. How. Did. You guys. Find out. About this place?" I then paused and gestured to them, to make it more obvious that I was speaking to them and was hoping they'd respond.

After a beat, Dean cleared his throat. "Well, actually, we were on our way to a camping spot an hour or so from here when the car battery died." He spoke in a deep and measured tone.

"Oh, he's such a kidder," Soraya said, slapping his knee gently. "That's the plot of one of my favorite movies."

I could tell from the look on Dean's face that it wasn't one of his faves.

"Scary?" I asked.

Her eyes grew wide. "AMAZINGLY scary! Angry ghosts. Poltergeists. Monsters. I can't watch it alone."

"My new bride has a soft spot for scary stuff," Dean said.

I knew I liked her. "So is that why you're here?"

Soraya nodded quickly. "I heard about this place from a friend whose father or uncle—or maybe it was a great-uncle—tried to make it through way back when. The story is that just being here turned his hair white!"

"I think that was old age, dear," said Dean the unimaginative.

"Anyway," she continued, "since it's our honeymoon—"

"HONEYMOON!" I almost leapt out of my seat in excitement.

Soraya's eyes darted around and quivered so much she looked like she might break apart. "You scared me!"

"Sorry," I said, sitting back down. "I can apparently be a little intense sometimes. I was just so excited because you said you were on your honeymoon, and I've got friends who are about to get married." My chattering seemed to calm her down, so I went on. "OMG. Congratulations! Gabe, they just got married!"

She smiled at me and flashed her ring.

"Lovely. His sister"—I indicated Gabe over my shoulder—"is about to have a wedding. I have so many questions for you. First, what kind of cake did you have?"

But then Bertie came back in, pushing an old cart. The wheels squeaked and screeched. It sounded like the wailing of a ghost.

CHAPTER 6

CHARLOTTE'S WORLD

The cart looked dusty, much like the TV sitting on it. The TV was cased in very ugly wood panels. If the idea was to have it blend in with the rest of the decor, it didn't work.

"Let's table this convo for now," I said.

Soraya nodded, but Dean didn't react.

Bertie said, "I was trying to explain it all from memory, but I forgot we have a video!"

I motioned for Gabe to come sit with us. We settled ourselves in the armchairs, and Bertie turned the cart to face us. She pressed a button on the front, and the TV turned on. It was *ancient*—the kind with a built-in VCR—and it was *loud*. She opened a case about the size of a hardcover book, then pulled out a videotape and popped it in the slot at the bottom of the TV. White, gray and black flecks danced around for a second, emitting a high-pitched electric squeal that made my ears hurt. The VCR clicked and whirred, then the static on the TV rearranged itself into recognizable shapes.

A woman stood in front of Glyndebourne Manor. She was wearing long orange pants that flared at the bottom, a dark brown turtleneck and a floral bandanna that seemed right out of *Scooby-Doo*. She held a small microphone and had twisted the cord around her index finger. She tossed her head and fluffed out her pouffy hair, then smacked her lips. She looked very glam.

"Are we rolling? Yes? Okay, great." Fuzzy bars of static waved down the screen, making the whole thing very creepy and sort of hard to make out.

"Behind me is the most disturbing haunted house in the world," she began in a serious, melodramatic voice. "A host of specters, ghouls, phantoms and poltergeists await you inside. But also, some of the most beautifully haunting art, music and design ever created. Glyndebourne Manor was built by the world-famous Charlotte Scherrer.

"This is Charlotte's world.

"A warning: The house has many tricks up its sleeves— much like Charlotte herself.

"This is Charlotte's story."

I looked over at Gabe, and he was already looking at me. We widened our eyes in excitement and gave each other a thumbs-up.

Old photos appeared on-screen, including one of an unsmiling child at a sewing machine, putting the finishing touches on an incredibly ornate gown.

"From an early age," the narrator continued, "Charlotte had a genius for design. When she was just a girl, she created and made the dresses for the world premiere of the opera *The Tale of Tsar Saltan*. The show was soon forgotten, but the costumes had caught the eye of opera companies around the world. Chicago. New York. Then Milan, Paris, London.

"When Charlotte was just thirty-one, the Moscow Art

Theatre commissioned her for a groundbreaking production of *Boris Godunov*."

"That's one of the costumes over there!" Gabe exclaimed. He'd produced a pad and pencil from some pocket in his pants and was taking notes.

"Cool," I said.

Dean, I noticed, was nodding off.

"But Charlotte hungered for more. She studied set design, engineering, even magic. And soon, she was a master of all. She designed the sets, the costumes, the lighting, the staging—even the programs—for a string of smashing successes: *The Barber of Seville, Tosca, Aida*."

Gabe jotted down the names. "More operas that match the costumes over by the—"

"Wait!" I said. "I can tell this is about to get really interesting!"

"It launched her into superstardom. The sets were so ingenious that the techniques she used to make them are still a mystery today.

"But whispers began: How could one woman so quickly become so skilled? Some said she had struck a deal . . . with the devil."

Gabe gulped.

My eyes widened, and I leaned closer in my chair, not wanting to miss a single second of the Good Stuff.

Dean snored.

"Despite the snide comments," continued the woman on TV, "Charlotte remained the most in-demand and highest-paid designer in the world. Soon, she founded her own production company, which toured more than thirty countries. Her final triumph, a staging of *The Magic Flute* in Vienna, has never been surpassed."

The screen showed an image of a huge dome painted like a starry night sky with a woman at the center, standing in a fluffy cloud.

"That's the Queen of the Night's aria scene," said Gabe.

"The one you mentioned in the car? It's beautiful."

"Told you," he said with a small smile.

"Suddenly, at the pinnacle of her success, she stopped," the narrator explained. "To this day, no one knows the reason. Charlotte withdrew from the public eye. She bought this plot of land and began the decades-long construction of the grand house you now see behind me.

"But more rumors swirled. The house was cursed. Charlotte was a witch.

"Were the stories true? Had she opened a portal to the spirit realm that, like Pandora's box, could never be closed?"

"I hope so," I said to Gabe, who was back to scribbling furiously.

"No one has been able to uncover its secrets, not even her family. And I should know—I'm her great-grandniece!" The woman winked and flashed a huge toothy smile, then cleared her throat and got back into it.

"Every twenty-five years, the manor's doors open—"

Bertie leaned over and hit the fast-forward button. "A lot of this was in the email," she said. The woman on-screen seemed to spin in triple speed for a minute before Bertie hit play again.

". . . before time runs out at midnight on November 1, the moment All Hallows' Eve ends. If you find yourself too terrified, every room has a button that will summon someone to come get you and escort you off the premises. On the second night, you will be collected by one of the grounds-keepers—maybe me! (another smile)—and you will attend dinner with your fellow contestants in the banquet hall. That is, if you can last that long. If you succeed—although no one has yet!—you will be rewarded with untold riches, and just maybe the secrets to one of the greatest minds our world has ever known. Stay sharp, stay smart, and yes, stay scared. It will be your way to survive. But now—to begin!"

She waved her arms again and smiled another TV-presenter smile that didn't quite match the tone of her speech. A voice offscreen said, "Cut!" and she relaxed. "I'm so sick of this spiel. How was that? Was that okay?" But before we could hear the reply, the video stopped and we were suddenly staring at a blue screen.

Dean woke with a start. "Was that it?" he asked.

"Well, yeah," said Bertie. "They made this video back in the seventies to explain some things. I just forgot about it. This is my first time completely in charge. That woman on the tape was my mom. The whole family gets involved. Like I said, Charlotte never married or had kids, so we're descended from her brother."

I was about to ask why the family was still hanging around this place after a hundred years when Bertie clapped her hands.

"Now! On to the big event!"

"What event?" I asked. Neither the email nor the video had specified what the first step would be. "Don't we just head to our rooms now?"

"I got ahead of myself earlier. There's still the performance!" she said. "Please sit." She pointed to the table under the windows. "I'm going to turn off the lights."

Gabe and I sat down next to each other on one side of the table, facing the windows. Dean sat next to us, and Soraya positioned herself at one end. Bertie pressed the old light switch, and we were suddenly in complete darkness. Gabe grabbed my hand and gripped it.

"Yowch!" I said.

"Sorry," he whispered and loosened his grip, but he didn't let go.

Bertie lit a candle, and a very small circle of flickering light illuminated her face. She walked over to the table and sat down in the middle chair across from us, with her back to the windows. She held the candle below her chin, as if she were telling a scary story at a sleepover.

"Well, folks, welcome to our little 'escape the haunted house' challenge. Before I can take you to your rooms, we must ask the spirits if they'll allow you to stay."

CHAPTER 7

THE PORTRAIT IN THE LIBRARY

"Do I really have to sit through a seance?" Dean asked.

"In a way, Dan," said Bertie, a bit annoyed. "You'll see. I have just a bit more to get through, if you don't mind."

Dean nodded and turned to Soraya, who smiled at him.

"Okay. Where was I?" said Bertie. "The spirits, yes. Now, please join hands and close your eyes. This should take only a moment."

Soraya giggled nervously and closed her eyes, placing her hands on the table, palms up. Dean shook his head but did the same, joining his hand with Soraya's on

55

the table. I took his right hand and brought up Gabe's hand and my own so they were on the table too. Bertie took Gabe's other hand so we were all linked together.

"This is *so cool*," I whispered to Gabe.

"This is so *creepy*," he whispered back.

I felt his hand tremble slightly in mine. Then I closed my eyes.

When Bertie spoke again, her voice was different: huskier, deeper. "Dear spirits, will you grant entry to these guests in your abode? Spirits, do you hear our call?"

Bertie paused. There was a slight chill, and even with my eyes closed, I could tell the candle had gone out.

Dean snorted. "So is that a yes?"

"Silence, please," said Bertie. She relit the candle, cleared her throat and began again. "Spirits, do you hear our call? Will you let these people stay?"

I felt a gush of cold wind and opened one eye. Behind Bertie, one of the windows was ajar. I gasped.

"What is it?!" Gabe opened his eyes and saw the window. He gasped too. "Zed, do you think—"

"That it was ghosts?! I HOPE so!"

"Okay, guys, let's regroup," said Bertie, sounding a little flustered.

And then I saw it: a ghostly face, floating in the window. Forgetting my hands were intertwined on both sides, I raised my arm to wave, yanking Dean's arm with me.

"Ouch! What now?" he asked.

"The window! She was in the window! I saw her!" I'd seen a flash of white—a woman's face.

Bertie turned sharply. "Really? Where?" she said, clearly surprised.

"She . . . she was right behind you. But she's not there anymore. She's . . . she's gone."

Gabe looked at me and frowned. "Zed, are you sure?"

"I swear! She was right there!"

"Was it *Charlotte*?" he asked in an awed whisper, looking up at the portrait, which was barely visible in the gloom.

"Yes! Or . . . no, it was someone else. It was . . . ugh, I don't know!"

"It's her! She's here!" screamed Soraya.

We all tried to look around.

Bertie stood up. "I'm going to turn the lights back on. This is too much," she said, but before she'd even taken a step, there was a thunderously loud *CRASH* and a splintering *CRACK*.

Bertie turned, the candle held out in front of her. The portrait of Charlotte had fallen from over the mantel and landed face down on the ground. The frame had split, and splinters of wood were scattered across the floor.

"Oh no!" I gasped, running over to see the damage.

In the dim light of Bertie's candle, I saw that the force of impact with the ground had pushed the canvas forward through its frame, ripping the brown paper backing. And in that rip, I saw something poking out. I didn't touch it

58

at first, in case it was a piece of wood or something sharp. Instead, I brushed my fingers across the paper in the frame, feeling the edges of the rip. Then, gingerly, I touched the rip itself. It wasn't sharp at all, but there was definitely something between the painting and the paper. I lifted the paper up carefully, revealing a small rectangle, maybe cardboard.

Bertie turned the lights on. My eyes adjusted. Everyone got up to join me around the portrait.

"Is she okay?" Gabe murmured.

"I guess that's a no on us staying," said Dean.

"A priceless work of art has been damaged, Dan," Bertie snapped. "Cut it out with the jokes."

"It's *Dean*!" he said.

She ignored him and turned to me. "Zed, be careful! There are splinters all around there. You could get hurt!"

But I'd already grabbed the rectangle and pulled it free. It was a piece of thick sketchbook paper, about the size of a tablet. I turned it over. There was a drawing on the other side. The image was exactly the same as the portrait, except Charlotte was holding a book.

"Whoa! Look at this!" I turned to where Dean, Soraya and Gabe were standing, a few paces back from the portrait. Soraya walked closer.

"Is that . . . a book she's holding?" she asked.

"It *must* be. The ghost I saw wanted us to find this! She was being helpful!"

"Ghosts aren't real," said Dean.

"Whatever, Dan," I said, but then I looked at Gabe, who had turned as pale as a ghost himself. I sighed. "He's probably right, though, Gabe. It was probably just gravity."

Gabe seemed to calm down a little bit.

I looked at the sketch again. Charlotte was definitely holding a book. It was closed with a clasp and decorated with some kind of weird eye motif. I showed it to Gabe.

"Oh, birch bark!" he said, pointing to the eyes.

"Not eyes?"

He smiled. "Birch bark sometimes looks like eyes, but no, that's definitely birch. See the horizontal markings?"

I studied it. "Actually, yeah."

"Could it be a clue?" he said.

We looked around at the shelves, but we didn't see any books that looked like the one in the sketch.

"What does this have to do with *anything*?" said Dean.

Soraya turned to him. "Come *on*, honey. I've made you watch so many horror movies at this point. *Obviously*, this is a clue."

To my surprise, Gabe spoke up, rocking on the balls of his feet like he always does when he's nervous. "Also, you know what?" he said. "Birch bark is cool anyway. I don't need it to be a clue. Sometimes it's fun just to *learn* stuff!"

Before we could argue anymore, we heard three clear knocks from the table we'd been sitting at. Gabe jumped and squealed. Soraya gasped.

"Well, Dean, *that* is a yes," said Bertie. "And it also signals it's time to call it a night."

I stamped my foot three times on the carpet to tell the ghosts I appreciated it.

Bertie turned to us. "I'll show you and Gabe to your room first, and you can prepare to start your investigations."

Gabe was shivering next to me. "Maybe we should go home now? This is getting too scary."

I put my hand on his shoulder. "You've just gazed upon five of the coolest opera costumes your geeky eyes have ever seen, right?"

He looked back at the glass cases.

"So just imagine the awesomeness that awaits inside. What are a few ghosts when art is on the menu? Also, 'encore.'"

He relented. "All right, show us the way."

"I'll protect you from any ghosts," I said, doing my best to imitate Sam flexing her biceps. That got a laugh out of Gabe.

I handed the sketch to Bertie. She placed it carefully on the wooden table near the window. The eyes seemed to be staring at us, even when we began to walk away.

"Righto," said Bertie. "On our way." And she walked toward the secret passage, beckoning us to follow.

Gabe pulled out his notebook and doodled the birch pattern from the book's cover, then pocketed it again.

Bertie pushed a carved grape in a big carved vine, and the secret panel door opened. We stepped into a short passageway. Bertie pointed to a door on our right. "That's the banquet hall—I showed it to Dean and Soraya earlier, but it's getting late and I have the feeling you two will see it soon." She winked. "We're going back out to the left." She opened that door, and we stepped into the foyer again.

"Ooh, a shortcut!" I said. "An essential haunted house feature."

My mind was racing. We had a little more than forty-eight hours to solve the coolest escape rooms ever in a super haunted house filled with secret passages. I still held on to the hope we could do it in less time than that. But first, we needed to find this mysterious book. Why else would the ghost have shown us the sketch?

I also needed to keep Gabe from running for the exits. If all went well, we'd meet some ghosts, we'd win the money for Sam and Jo, and I'd still make it home in time for Count Dracula to get some full-size chocolate bars on Halloween night.

I looked over at Gabe. "We got this. Everything is coming up Zed."

CHAPTER 8

SUN ROOM

Bertie led us up the staircase, pausing on the landing to double-check a worn and folded piece of paper she pulled from her pocket. She clicked her tongue and looked up the left side of the stairs. "Yep, it's this way. Sorry, I don't come in here often."

"You don't live here?" I asked as we kept ascending the staircase. Like most things in the house so far, it was much larger than it looked at first glance.

"Nope. The house doesn't let people in most of the time."

"You talk about the house like it's a person," said Gabe, reaching for my hand to help me up the last step.

"If it's a person, it's a cranky old person. Old habits die hard. Or maybe they died and are now haunting me," she chuckled. "This way," she said, looking at her paper again and pointing right down a long hallway. "I don't really believe in all this ghost stuff, but I grew up in a family where they always talked like that. I can't deny, though, that when you're in the house, you *feel* something, a presence. And it *is* true that the house has a complex system of locks and mechanics—at least, I assume that's what's happening. The house opens once every month—and even then, it opens only a few rooms. I've never been able to explore the entire place. No one has, except Charlotte."

"Wait, really? *No one* has? Not even your mom, in the video?" I asked.

She shook her head. "My mom almost never came into the house at all. She was too afraid. Even before she passed on, I was the one who did most of the work."

"But only once a month?" asked Gabe.

"Well, that's just the main house. I also take care of the grounds. I have a small cabin about a ten-minute walk from here, in a stand of birch trees. Really lovely, actually. And much more manageable than this giant place. I can't imagine living here and having to take care of it all."

"Lots to maintain?" asked Gabe.

"Well, these days, nothing is working like it should—don't step there, Zed!" She grabbed my hand and directed me away from a spot on the floor. "The boards in that spot are rotting. I need to replace them."

Gabe and I exchanged a glance.

"Like the porch steps?" said Gabe.

Bertie nodded. "There are a lot of repairs to do. It's intense prepping for this contest and trying to keep the house in a state of readiness."

"Like Thornfield Hall," I said.

"*Jane Eyre*, huh? You read a lot, don't you?"

I took a deep breath and was about to tell Bertie all about *The Monster's Castle* when Gabe cut in. "Do *not* get them started on Gothic novels. They'll never stop, and I want to go to sleep sometime this century."

"Says the guy who can talk about opera until the cows come home."

"Well, you've certainly come to the right house for that," said Bertie.

"There are cows?!" said Gabe, not able to contain his excitement. This guy and his nature obsession.

"No, I meant because of the opera. Cows would be too much work. I do have a pretty nice vegetable garden near my cabin, though."

"Wait, can I see it?" said Gabe.

"Can we get back to the scary mystery and the mysterious presence in this house?" I asked.

Bertie laughed. "I don't know what else there is to say. All right, here we are."

We had stopped at the end of the hallway in front of a dark wooden door with a small sun painted on it. She unhooked her ring of keys from her belt. It had at least ten small identical keys on it. She flicked through them until she found one with a small sun symbol, and then she unlocked the door and pushed it open.

"After you."

Gabe and I stepped inside, and Bertie came in behind us.

"This is where you'll be staying tonight. There's a water closet attached."

"What's a water closet?" I asked.

"Oh, it's an old term from the turn of the last century. It means there's a room with a toilet and a sink, but no shower or bathtub. People also called it a WC."

"Good thing we showered before we got in the car," I said.

"And that Sam didn't toss her cookies all over us," Gabe added.

"Man, you kids sure are something," Bertie chuckled. "The bathtubs in the house are all separate from the toilets. It's a weird quirk of old houses. But other rooms you'll visit will have a full bathroom *and* water closet, just not this one."

In the middle of the room was a large bed with four posts and a bedside table. It looked like Lysander's bed in *The Monster's Castle*!

Bertie saw me looking at it. "Hope you don't mind sleeping in the same bed. It's big, though, and you should each have plenty of room. Remember, don't go back through this door again." She jerked her thumb at the door we'd just come through. "If you need me, press this button." She pointed to a small sun-shaped button near the light switch. "This is for non-ghost-related emergencies. Medical emergencies or anything like that. You won't get kicked out of the competition for that kind of call. Now, if you get too scared and you want to quit the challenge entirely, press the sun button three times in a row. Any questions?"

I opened my mouth, but Gabe cut me off. "Nothing, thanks. We're okay."

"All right! I guess I'll go get Dean and Soraya settled." She sighed. "See ya when I see ya." She gave us a salute and left.

Gabe turned to me. "I'm tired, Zed. I don't want to ask questions right now—I just want to sleep."

I had to admit, I was tired too. Looking at how comfy the bed was made me realize I was exhausted.

Even if I had wanted to keep exploring, there wasn't much to see. It was a small room. The walls were painted a pale gold, and there was nothing on them. The room was lit by two small-ish sconces set into the walls—one near the light switch by the door and one on the far wall, next to the door that led to the bath-room (or I guess just the "room," since there was no bath). I couldn't see how high the ceiling was because the lamplight didn't reach that far. I put my bag down and went to the side of the bed with the table.

"Can I have this side?" I asked Gabe. "I want to look at my night-light."

"Yeah, go ahead."

We took turns in the WC, changing into our pj's and brushing our teeth. (I had purple footie pajamas patterned with colored pumpkins and jack-o'-lanterns.) Gabe got into bed first and immediately plunged face down into his pillow. I tried to climb in, too, but it was just a bit too high to swing my leg over.

"A little help?" I asked Gabe.

He grumbled into the pillow but reached out his hand and helped pull me up. I put my pumpkin night-light on the table and switched it on. It emitted a comforting warm glow.

68

"Goodnight, Gabe," I whispered to his side of the bed. "Goodnight, Willoughby," I whispered to the night-light. "Good night, ghosts," I whispered to the air.

"Zed, I'm trying to sleep," mumbled Gabe.

I closed my eyes and let Willoughby light the room in his small way.

CHAPTER 9

PICTURE PERFECTIONIST

I woke up. It was still dark. "Gabe? Are you awake?" But he didn't answer. Willoughby was still shining on my night-stand, but I couldn't see much beyond his small circle of light. There wasn't a window. I cursed myself for not asking Bertie how we would tell when it was daytime. I wished I had a flashlight.

I scooted close to the edge of the bed to pick up Willoughby to light my way to the WC. I'd almost reached him, but when I tried to scoot a bit closer, I ran out of mattress space. I rolled off the bed, smacking my butt hard on the floor.

"AUGH!" I yelled.

Gabe gasped awake. "Who's there?!"

"It's me, genius." I tried to lower my voice. I said a bit hoarsely, "Sorry, I fell off the bed."

"I was actually sleeping well for once," Gabe said and rolled over.

From my new spot on the floor, I could see that Willoughby's light faintly reached the wall, hitting the glass of the picture frames and giving them a pleasant orange tint.

Wait. Picture frames?

"Gabe," I whispered. "Are you still awake?"

He groaned. "Yes. Unfortunately."

"Do you remember what was on the walls when we came in?"

"What is this, some messed-up memory game?" He thought for a second. "Nothing was on the walls. Why are you even asking?"

"Because," I said in a hushed whisper, "there's . . . *stuff* on the walls now."

Gabe sat bolt upright. "*What?!*"

I stood up and rubbed my sore backside. "Where's the light switch?"

"Near the door, I think."

I walked toward where I thought the light switch was, but my stylish pajama-ed feet were too slippery on the wooden floor and I almost fell again.

"Hang on, Zed." I heard Gabe briefly shuffle, and then he shone a flashlight over my shoulder.

"Wait, even your pajamas have pockets?! And you slept with *that* in them?"

"No, that would be uncomfortable." He paused. "It was under my pillow."

"Nice." I turned the lights on, and we both screamed.

The *entire room* was different. Gone were the bare walls; instead, they were absolutely *covered* in identically sized picture frames. There were dozens—maybe even hundreds— over the doors and all the way down to the mantelpiece. I jumped again.

"There's a *mantelpiece?*"

Across from the bed there was now a wooden mantelpiece. Usually, a mantelpiece would come with a fireplace, but there was nothing there—only a blank section of wall where the fireplace would have gone. And above the mantelpiece was a huge mirror. I waved to my reflection. My mirror self waved back.

"Hello, mirror ghosts!" I said. No answer. I slumped my shoulders. I'd been hoping it was some kind of haunted mirror, but no such luck. Just my stylish reflection looking back at me, with Gabe cowering in bed behind me, covers pulled up to his chin. I went closer to the mantel and crouched down, remembering how I'd found the secret sketch by touching the painting. Maybe there were secrets here too? I ran my hand all around the wall, feeling for cracks or squishy spots.

"What are you doing?" Gabe asked.

"I'm trying to find secret compartments."

"You might not be able to tell just from touching it. Knock on it. Normal walls don't make as loud a sound as hollow ones."

"Gabe, you're a genius. How did you know that?"

He looked down at the blanket and fiddled with it a bit,

but he was smiling. "I guess I do have my moments," he said. "I've looked at a lot of old houses with my dad. He taught me that."

I knocked across the wall under the mantelpiece. It was muffled. Then, right in the center, I heard it. Hollow.

"Whoa!" I knocked again. Again, a louder sound. Like knocking on the front of an empty drawer. "Open sesame!" I said, doing my best magician-like hand flourish. Nothing. "Please open!" Again, nothing.

Gabe got out of bed and knelt down next to me. He looked closely at the wall and knocked again. "Hmm." He stood up, then tapped it with his foot. "Oh, look at this."

I rose to see what he was looking at. On the top of the mantelpiece, there were five rectangular pedestals only slightly higher than the rest of the mantel. They were small, about the size of—

"Picture frames!" I yelled out.

"Huh?"

"The picture frames, Gabe! I'd bet anything these stands are the same size as those picture frames!"

He looked at the frames, then back at the mantel. "Let me try something," he said. He grabbed a frame off the wall, then set it down on one of the stands. There was a loud clunk, and the pedestal lowered until the picture frame rested just above the wood of the mantel.

"Whoa!" I picked the frame back up. The same clunk sounded, and the pedestal rose again. I looked at the picture in my hand. It was an old black-and-white photo with four people facing the camera: two men and two women. There was a man sitting in a chair in the foreground, wearing a top hat and a black overcoat, and he had very dramatic stage makeup on. The other people in the picture were dressed more simply, kind of like Charlotte in her portrait. In fact . . . I squinted, scrutinizing the woman on the far left standing behind the seated man.

"Gabe, doesn't that look like Charlotte?" I pointed to her.

74

"Yeah, maybe," he said, studying her face.

"Wait, let's check the back," I said, turning the frame around to see if it had any clues like the portrait did. There was no outline or shape indicating something else was inside the frame, but it did have an inscription: *L→R: TOSCA: C.S., F.D., H. Beach, P. Dell, Milan, 1901.*

"C.S.—Charlotte Scherrer!" I pumped my fist in the air. "But what does T-O-S-C-A stand for?"

"Let me see," said Gabe, taking it from me and flipping between the photo and the inscription. "No, it says *Tosca*. I think this is Charlotte with part of the cast or crew of the opera *Tosca*, listed from left to right, 'L to R.'"

I groaned. "So nothing cool. No ghosts. Just more opera. Great."

"If it's in Milan, I bet they were there to perform at La Scala! That's the opera house that the design of—"

"Yeah, that this house is based on. I do remember that. But what do Charlotte's vacation pictures have to do with anything?"

Gabe passed me the photo again. I studied it. It seemed like a pretty normal old photo. The background was indistinct, but they were inside somewhere.

Gabe knitted his brows. "I don't know."

"Also, it says 'C.S.' and 'F.D.' But then the other names are more spelled out. I wonder what that means. Could that be a clue?" I asked.

"Clue or not, I think we know what we have to do, right?" Gabe asked.

"You mean, put five frames on the mantelpiece and see what it does?"

"Exactly," said Gabe, smiling.

"I bet it will open that secret drawer," I said, pointing to the panel under the mantel.

"I'm not sure what will happen, but let's see if any of the other photos have writing on them," suggested Gabe.

We both looked around the room. The walls were covered with frames as far as the eye could see.

"Okay, let's try it," I said. "You take the right side, I'll take the left."

He nodded, and we got to work.

I took down as many frames as I could fit in my arms and sat on the floor with them spread out in front of me. Gabe went one by one, flipping over each photo and studying it before placing it back. "I don't want to disturb any of them, just in case," he said when he caught me staring. I liked my method better because I could sit down and focus my attention on each.

The photos were all black and white. Those that had dates written on the back were from the early 1900s. Most had Charlotte in them, but not all. There were a couple that were just silly framed postcards, like one that had an illustration of dogs wearing monks' robes in a church-looking place with the caption "Laboratory: An oratory for Labradors." I showed Gabe and he laughed, but I didn't totally get it.

At one point, Gabe called me over to look at one he'd found near the mantelpiece, where the *Tosca* photo was. It was a framed program for an opera called *La Bohème* from 1903.

"One of my favorites," said Gabe.

"But what's so special about it?"

"It's the incredible story of these starving artists, and—"

"Not the opera, the program! Why am I looking at this?"

"Well, there aren't any other framed playbills that I can see. It might be significant."

"I can't reach it. Can you get it down?"

He stretched his arm and grabbed it. We gave it a closer inspection. The program had a dozen or so signatures on it surrounding a drawing of a woman holding a candle. She looked sad.

"A souvenir?" Gabe suggested. "I guess she worked on this one?"

I pointed to a specific signature that wasn't only a name: "*Brava to the best friend I could have wished for. F.D.*"

"'F.D.,'" I said. "Wasn't that on the *Tosca* photo too?"

Gabe checked. "Yeah. Good eye."

"I have to put back some of those joke postcards. Look for more F.D. photos, and I'll see if there are any more programs over on my side."

As I put back the postcards, a photo near the bedside table caught my eye: a woman was standing on a theater stage wearing a poofy hat and a cloak emblazoned with suns and stars. She was tall, with curly hair sticking out from under her hat. She was waving a wand out toward the audience, and at the tip of the wand was a blurry spray of sparks. In the lower left was an autograph: "*To C., the source of the magic. I.e., love always.*" I studied the photograph before taking it off the wall. The woman looked oddly familiar. I assumed the "C" of the autograph meant Charlotte. And "love always" . . . well, my romance-o-meter was buzzing.

Zed Watson is many things: intrepid literary detective, fashion icon (although many disagree), monster expert (vampires rule!!!), but most of all, a romantic. *The Monster's Castle* had a vampire-werewolf romance that drew me in, and one of the reasons Gabe and I were even here was to give Sam and Jo the wedding of their dreams. I leaned in closer to the photo and read the writing again. *I.e., love always.* One thing I knew, deep in my pint-sized soul: romance was afoot.

I took the photo off the wall and turned it around, eager to see the inscription. But there was only a date and two initials: "F.D., 1907."

"Another F.D. photo," I said.

Gabe walked over. "Found something?"

"Not sure. But it sort of called to me. It's weird—we found that program and two photos with 'F.D.' on them, but no connection between the three, except that Charlotte worked on the operas and likely made this awesome costume." I indicated the starry cloak and hat.

Gabe picked up the photo and sat down on the bed to inspect it. I sat next to him.

"Hmm," he said. "I don't think this is from an opera."

"But it's interesting for a different reason," I said. "Did you see the autograph? Did you see that it says '*I.e., love always*'? Love always. Do I sense romance in the air? Rather romantic to write to someone that they are 'the source of magic,'" I pointed out.

"You think everything is a romance, Zed," said Gabe.

"Maybe I think everything is a romance because it is. Love is all around us, Gabe." I paused. "Although I'll admit I don't know what 'i.e.' means."

"*Id est*," said Gabe.

"You dest? What's a 'dest'?"

"No, it's Latin. 'I.e.' stands for *id est*, which means 'that is.' 'I.e.' is the short form for 'another way of saying something.' It's sort of like 'in other words.' So whoever wrote this was saying 'You are the source of the magic. That is, love always.'" He thought for a moment. "But that doesn't feel correct. 'Love always' *isn't* really another way of saying 'You are the source of the magic.' You see what I mean?"

I nodded. "You just had a real dictionary moment there. I'm so glad we're friends." He smiled. "I think I get what you're saying, though. Like, she could have just written 'You are the source of the magic, love always.' The 'i.e.' doesn't add anything here. It just confuses the message."

"Right," agreed Gabe. "It feels like I'm missing something. Also, if Charlotte and this person were in love, why didn't she write something on the back? Like who this person is, or a heart or some other love note?"

I stroked my chin. "Well, there's no way to tell, but . . . F.D. again. It feels like more than a coincidence—i.e., this seems like the sort of thing we should be looking for."

"Nice Latin usage," said Gabe, smiling.

"Thank you. I learned from the best." I looked again at the magician's face. "I could swear I've seen her face before . . ."

"Maybe she's her friend or she's related to her somehow. Wait!" he exclaimed. I almost saw a light bulb appear above his head. "Have you seen any photos of Charlotte's family so far? Her siblings, nieces, nephews, parents, that sort of thing?"

"No. Not even anyone who looks like her. Those eyes . . . haunting." I clasped my hands together.

He rolled his own eyes. "I mean, have *any* of the photos been of Charlotte at her house, or *any* house, with anyone who could be a family member? Any photos of her *not* at work?"

"What are you getting at?"

"Earlier, you asked what Charlotte's vacation photos had to do with anything. But none of these *are* vacation photos. I haven't seen a single photo of her just hanging out."

"And you think that's significant?"

"Yes. And I think F.D. is a classic red herring."

"What do you mean?"

"We'd have to pull every single picture off these walls just to find some photos with 'F.D.' written on the back. I think there's a different pattern here. A much more specific one."

"Like what?"

"Her career. That's the key."

"Are you sure?"

He paused and looked around in wonder at the photos again. Then he turned back to me. I liked watching him put the pieces together like Sherlock Holmes.

"Let's start with this photo of the magician here. I would bet she's wearing a costume made by Charlotte. And then the one we saw of the cast of *Tosca*—all the photos I've seen so far are Charlotte at work and/or Charlotte's work. In a theater, at the opera and so on. There's even one of her at her workshop over there. When you put them together, it's like a career timeline."

"And?"

"Well, there are five spots on the mantelpiece, right?"

"And???"

"And we put that first frame down and something moved. So we're assuming that we need to put down five frames, right?"

"Gabe, what are you *saying*?"

"What if we need to find five photos that are, like, the five most important career moments, maybe in order from oldest to newest? That's what all the dates could be for!"

I thought about it, then looked around the room at all the pictures again. He was right—they weren't vacation photos after all. She lived and breathed her work.

"You might be on to something there. But how do we narrow it down?"

He furrowed his brow, thinking hard. Then he smacked his hand on his forehead. "Oh, we are *so* clueless."

"Wait, I thought we were gathering clues!"

"No, I mean the costumes!"

"What costumes? Do I need to be looking only for photos with costumes in them?"

82

"No, Zed, *the* costumes."

Suddenly, I got it. "From the library! The display cases!" We high-fived and then low-fived.

"Exactly. And there were only five. Five costumes, five operas, five pedestals. And the photos here all have dates on the back! So let's find photos of the five operas and put them in order according to the dates."

"I'm having a zone-out Zed moment. You don't remember what operas those costumes were from, do you?"

"Zed, please. Of course I remember. And I also wrote it all down." He dug through the pockets of his pants on the floor and pulled out his notepad triumphantly. "Got it!"

"Okay, what operas were the library costumes from?"

He dramatically flipped through the pages, then landed on the right spot, cleared his throat and started rattling off a list of bizarre words: "*Tosca, Aida, Boris Godunov—*"

"Wait, slow down. Boris what-do-enough?"

"Go-due-nov. They mentioned these operas by name in the video. Did you miss that part?"

"The video was all about ghosts and stuff! And how she made a pact with the devil!"

Gabe sighed. "Sure, but it was also about the operas she worked on. Anyway, *Boris Godunov*. It's a name. It's Russian. That was the costume that was a really huge and thick fur cloak."

"That one was pretty cool. Wait, what was the one that had, like, scales or something? It was really green."

"Oh, that was Papageno—or his wife, Papagena—from *The Magic Flute*! You know, it goes . . . 'Ba-da-*da twittle-eet-tee-tee*! Bah da *dah* da-*da* da da da *dun* da *da*.'" He whistled a couple of bars.

I dragged my fingers down my face. "No more, Gabe! Please stop making those sounds with your mouth! *Why* does it sound like a screechy bird?"

"Because he *is* a bird! He's a parrot. It's supposed to sound like that."

"It's supposed to sound bad? Opera is the worst. I fear I will never truly understand you, good buddy." I shook my head. "But okay, so *Tosca*—check. *Aida*, *Boris Got-under*, *Magic Flute*? What else do we got?"

Gabe ran his finger down his list. "*The Barber of Seville*."

"Now you're just making these up."

He huffed in frustration. "No, and this is getting silly. Come on. Let's just look for those, okay? Any *Magic Flute*. Any *Aida*, *Boris Godunov* or *Barber of Seville*."

"Okay, I'll have another look. But no *La Bohème*?"

"No, that one wasn't included in the display cases downstairs or in the video. It was just the five: *Tosca*, *Aida*, *Boris*, *Magic Flute* and *Barber*. The ticket stub was another F.D. misdirection."

I looked back at my bedside table, where I'd put the *Bohème* frame. I didn't want to put it back on the wall just yet. I leaned over and placed the magician photo next to the *Bohème* program. Even if they weren't part of the solution, they could still be important. I noticed Willoughby was still on, so I turned him off to save battery power.

Gabe and I split up again, this time taking opposite sides to bring fresh eyes to the pics.

"I found *Aida*!" said Gabe a minute later. He hugged it to his chest. The back had the name of the woman wearing the costume ("P. Dell" again) and the date: 1905.

We hunted for a few more minutes. I had to admit, it was nice to be able to skim more quickly through all the frames. Soon, Gabe had finished scouring his side. In addition to the photo from *Aida* (Gabe's favorite, with that huge headpiece thing), we'd found *Boris* (it matched the fur cape thing from downstairs and had the date 1898) and a photo of Charlotte draping strips of feathered fabric on a mannequin, clearly building the Papageno costume. The back inscription said "For F.D., 1909."

"So the only thing that's left is her getting a haircut," I said.

Gabe shook his head ruefully. "Zed, it's not like that." He

walked to my side and scanned a bit more. "Found it!" He pointed to a photo of someone singing in front of an audience or something.

"Not even a barbershop quartet? What kind of opera is this?" I still wasn't convinced that opera wasn't the most boring thing on the planet.

Gabe smiled to himself. "Figaro here, Figaro there," he said, taking it off the wall. He turned it around and showed me the inscription on the back: "*Il Barbiere di Siviglia*, 1900."

"Wow, someone really can't spell." I pointed to how "barber" was written.

"It's the Italian title."

I looked at the backs of all five photos we were going to put on the mantelpiece. "Only three of these five inscriptions have 'F.D.'—*Aida* and the *Barber* don't. Looks like you were right."

He smiled. "Evidently, my dear Watson."

"But it still feels like a loose thread in the story of this seamstress." I looked again at the cast pictures and at the one of Charlotte in her studio. Something nagged in the back of my brain. I was going to study the photos some more—maybe even ask Gabe if he had a pocket magnifying glass—but he took them from my hands.

"No time to waste, remember? Think of Halloween. Let's put these in order and celebrate the amazing career of Charlotte Scherrer."

We double-checked the dates of each one to make sure we had them in the right order.

"All right," said Gabe. "It's *Boris* from 1898, then *Barber* from 1900, then *Tosca* 1901, *Aida* 1905 and finally *Magic Flute* 1909."

We placed them in that order from left to right, then stepped back to watch them sink into the mantel.

As the first one lowered with a satisfying clunk, there was a sudden chill, a gust of cold wind.

It had taken me a moment to feel it because of my always warm pj's. I went to my side of the bed and grabbed my warmest sweater, then walked back to Gabe, throwing it over my head. I was still pulling it over my mop of hair and glasses when the final frame fell.

I pulled the sweater down and clapped my hands. "We did it!" I said. I glanced over at Gabe. He looked very pale.

"No, Zed. We didn't."

CHAPTER 10

F.D.

Gabe screamed and waved his arms, knocking my glasses off my face.

"Gabe? What is it?!" I reached down and searched for my glasses, putting them back on just in time to see him turning to run away.

"Encore! Come on!" I yelled, grabbing him before he could reach the door.

"A ghost! I saw it. I saw a ghost—"

"OMG! WHERE?!"

He pointed a shaking finger at the mantelpiece.

But before I could turn to look, the lights flickered and then went out. We weren't in complete darkness for long, though; an eerie glow now emanated from behind the panel under the mantelpiece. I watched, spellbound, as a hand reached out and around the panel.

Gabe screamed again and clutched his face, his eyes

squeezed shut. I blinked, and the hand disappeared. We were left in total darkness again. For a second, all was still, and then the mirror began to glow. I clasped my hands together in excitement—maybe the mirror was haunted after all!

There was a bright flash, and suddenly we were face to face with a REAL, ACTUAL GHOST. I could *almost* see the full shape of it—a tall floating specter, its eyes horribly sunken into its face and its mouth open in something like an eternal scream.

"Gabe! Gabe, look!" I tried to get him to open his eyes. The ghost suddenly stretched out its long spindly arm, and I could see bones in places where its flesh had rotted away. It pointed directly at me.

"HI!" I yelled.

Gabe whimpered.

Looking at the ghost with its outstretched arm, I was reminded of something I'd just seen. The magician! The woman with her hand outstretched, holding the wand!

I ran back to my bedside table, to the photos I had put there. I knew they would come in handy!

The ghost still hung in the air, floating, just pointing.

"I think we had it wrong, Gabe," I said. "We did need the F.D. pictures!" I picked up the *Bohème* frame and the magician photo and hugged them to my chest.

The ghost still didn't move as I snuck under it to replace the *Barber of Seville* picture with the *Bohème* program and *Aida* with the magician photo.

I placed them in order like he said. Now that the frames were all together, an electric shock ran through my brain. The reason I recognized the magician's face was because she was in all these photos. Only it was hard to tell because of all the makeup. In *Boris*, she was dressed as a man with a full beard, and in *Tosca*, she was playing a man as well, wearing a man's hat and cloak. But it was obviously her. It was even her in the illustration from *La Bohème*, dressed as a woman. You could see it was the same person.

"F.D., I presume," I said to her image as the frames began to sink into the mantelpiece once more. "But who are you?"

The same clunk, but this time the photos sank right into the wood . . . and another sound followed: a click from below the floating ghost.

The panel under the mantel slid away, revealing a crawl space that looked just big enough for us to fit through.

The ghost continued to float in front of the mantelpiece, hand still pointing at us, and Gabe chose that moment to open his eyes a crack. At the same time, the ghost opened its cavernous mouth even wider, unhinging its jaw, and let out a soul-rending shriek. It was *awesome*. Gabe also let out a scream that was almost on par with the ghost's.

"TIME TO GO, ZED! LET'S GO!" he yelled, getting down on all fours.

I pointed him forward like he was a blindfolded toddler heading toward a piñata. He scuttled along the floor while the ghost hovered in the air in front of the mirror, screaming and shrieking.

"Who are you, ghost?" I asked, looking directly into the disgusting sockets where its eyes had once been.

"ZED!!!!" screamed Gabe. He had almost made it through the crawl space and was reaching back for me. The ghost began to lower, wisps of hair and tattered cloth waving in the breeze. Its mouth opened again.

"What?! What are you trying to tell me?" I asked, but it didn't answer. It just kept moving its jaw up and down, shrieking and yelling.

"ZED, COME ON!"

I took a deep breath. Being haunted for real was extremely scary and awesome, but Gabe needed me. "Just a second, ghost," I said. "I need to get something."

I dashed over and grabbed our backpacks, then I got on my hands and knees and started scrambling for the exit. The ghost continued to shriek and move its jaw up and down, and I could feel its chill through my sweater.

I slid Gabe's backpack through the open panel.

"DON'T LOOK BACK, GABE!" I yelled into the hole. "NOT A PROBLEM."

I turned to speak to the specter one last time. "What's your message? Are you F.D.?" I asked, but it only screamed again. Then it reached for me, hands grasping the air.

"Yes! I knew we could be friends!"

I extended my hand, to wave or shake, to show that we were friendly to ghosts and would cooperate with whatever it needed, but then I felt a sharp tug as Gabe yanked me through the opening.

There was a click, and the panel slammed back into place, shutting us out forever. Gabe's hands still clutched my shoulder as I panted and peered around, trying to make out anything in the darkness.

CHAPTER II

THE HAUNTED HALLWAY

"I was trying to talk to the ghost!" I said, doing my best to escape Gabe's grip.

He responded—rudely, I thought—by tapping on the panel, making sure it was secure. There was the faintest light from somewhere behind us. Just enough to allow us to see each other's faces.

"Hmph," I said. "What if the ghost could have told us all the secrets of this place?"

"That thing broke through the wall like it wasn't even there!"

"And aren't you the least bit curious about how it did that?"

"No!" Gabe gave one final knock on the panel, then I heard him sit back, satisfied.

"Well, it can probably just come through the wall again anyway," I said. "It *is* a ghost."

Gabe yelped and scuttled away into the darkness.

I was now alone in what felt like the inside of a small box. Too cramped to stand up or move from side to side.

"Fine," I said. "I'll check out this place."

I reached my hands up. There was a ledge or shelf of some kind right above my head. I ran my hands along the edge and felt my fingertips touch something thin and rough. I wrapped my fingers around it and tugged. It came loose in my hand. Even in the gloom, I could tell it was a small book.

"Gabe, I think I found something."

"Me too," said Gabe. "Come over here."

I couldn't make him out in the darkness. "Where?"

"Crawl forward a little. I'm in a hallway."

I shoved the book in my backpack—we'd look at it later in better light—and shuffled forward. He was right. I emerged out of the little space into a very dim, very dingy and possibly very long hallway. There was only a single light, right above our heads, and then the rest of the hall was swallowed up in darkness just a few feet into the distance.

"Do you have that flashlight on you?"

He checked his pockets. "Shoot, I left it in the last room."

"With the ghost!" I said. "Darn it, I left Willoughby there too. Maybe the ghost can bring them to us?"

"I think we should go. That way," said Gabe, jerking his thumb behind him.

"You think this haunted hallway is less scary than that ghost?"

"Y-y-y-es," he shivered.

He wasn't shivering only with fear. The hallway was getting super cold. Even colder than the bedroom.

"Th-th-this place is—"

"SO COOL!" I said, beaming.

"N-n-ot the word I was l-l-looking for."

At that moment, something huge slammed into the panel behind us, and the whole hallway shook. Plaster came loose and landed on our shoulders like tiny snowflakes. The light above flickered.

"Hmmm. There must be a blocking spell on the panel," I said, frowning. "The ghost can't get through."

"G-g-g-good," Gabe said. A tiny puff of a cloud hovered in front of his face.

"Look, Gabe! A baby ghost."

"That's not a ghost. It's my breath."

"Chills might be a sign that another ghost is somewhere close."

"Chills are also a well-known sign of the flu."

"Good point, but I think this might be the beginning of a HAUNTING!" I clapped my hands. "I bet Charlotte had wicked parties here. Oooh, maybe we'll get to meet the ghosts of some really cool old movie stars!"

A cold mist began to ooze up from the floorboards.

I closed my eyes. "Come on, Clara Bow or Rudy Valentino, we're ready!"

"We . . . sh-sh-sh-should . . . mmmmmm-move," Gabe said, shivering.

"Fine. But first things first." I quickly unzipped my backpack and handed him a pullover. "Sam is always mocking my fashion choices, but see? Sweaters *are* practical. Arms up."

Gabe looked down at the picture on the front: a neon zombie unicorn having breakfast.

"Is that thing eating a bowl of brains?"

I grinned. "Because they're pink! Unicorns LOVE pink!"

"Um, maybe hypothermia isn't so bad."

I sighed and pulled the sweater over his head. "When the sweater warms up, the brains turn rainbow-colored."

"I can't wait."

The mist rose to the ceiling and twisted around the light bulb. There was a crackle, then a loud pop as the bulb exploded, throwing the hallway into complete darkness.

"Oh no," Gabe said.

"Now you won't be able to see the rainbow brains."

"We won't be able to see anything. Man, I wish I hadn't forgotten that flashlight."

"No time for regrets. There must be a door at the other end." I reached for his hand in the dark. "Let's go."

We took a loud step forward. The sound was quickly swallowed by the gloom.

"This is so amazing!"

"So creepy," Gabe said.

We took another tentative step forward. The floorboards creaked.

"Are your toes starting to hurt?" asked Gabe.

"Yes. I was hoping it was my feet being possessed by Fred Astaire or maybe the Nicholas Brothers!"

"Who?"

"You need to watch more old movies. I'd do a tap demonstration, but you can't see it. And sadly, my feet are not possessed."

"More likely frostbitten," Gabe said.

"Party pooper. Let's keep moving."

Two more steps, and the floor suddenly disappeared beneath my feet. I lurched forward and began to fall. Gabe pulled me backward, and we tumbled to the floor.

"Thanks! That was close," I said.

"Is there a hole there?"

"Yup. Let's see if I can figure out how big it is."

I got on all fours and felt around the freezing cold floor. "The floorboards just kind of end." I ran my hand along the edge. It was rough, as if the wood had splintered. "The ghosts here really do a number on wood," I said. "The gap stretches from wall to wall." I reached down as far as I could, but I didn't touch anything. "It's deeper than my arm anyway." I stretched forward. "And I can't feel the other side."

"So we're at a dead end?"

"An appropriate choice of words."

"But we can't head back—there's the ghost," Gabe squeaked.

"And we'd get kicked out. We'll have to jump."

"Jump? To where?"

"The other side."

"That's also a term for the afterlife, you know."

"I have an idea." I reached down and took off one of my sandals.

"Are you going to explain this idea, or do I have to guess?"

"Oh yeah! You can't see me. I'm going to throw something

as far as I think we can jump. If it lands, we're good. If it doesn't—hello, other side."

Before I could start overthinking, I took a deep breath and lobbed the sandal.

"Was that a puff sound?" Gabe asked.

"I was hoping for more of a clunk. But it did hit something! And the only way forward is that way."

"I still can't see you, but I assume you're pointing toward the hole."

"Past the hole. And I'm wearing only one sandal now and my foot is freezing. So let's go."

We took three big steps backward to get a running start.

"I'll go first," I said. "If you hear a scream . . . actually, I have no idea what you should do then."

"Nice speech."

"You know, if I die now, I'm going to seriously haunt you."

"I have no doubt."

"Here I go." I closed my eyes—not that they were doing much anyway—and ran forward.

Then I leapt.

Time seemed to stand still, with me frozen in midair for what felt like a lifetime, my heart racing as I wondered what was—or wasn't—under me and on the other side of the abyss.

Then my feet touched down on something soft and cold. I tumbled forward and landed in a pile of—

"SNOW!"

"Snow?"

I took a taste. "Yes. Soft, fluffy and wonderful. The Zed Watson of precipitation."

"Well, it's not ice cream, but I'll take it," he said.

Gabe's sneakers squeaked on the floor as he leapt through the air and landed safely near my feet.

"That was kinda cool," he said. "Find a door yet?"

"I was too busy making snow angels."

We inched forward slowly. I felt along in the air in front of me until my fingers touched something hard. I rapped it with my knuckles, and it made the lovely sound of fingers on wood.

"I'm surprised you could feel that," Gabe said. "I think my fingers are about to fall off."

He somehow found the doorknob and turned it. The door opened. Bright light suddenly flooded the hallway, and I turned away to shield my eyes.

There was a loud crack from behind us. I could barely make anything out in the blinding whiteness, but it looked like a large mouth was emerging from the hole behind us and gnawing at the floor. More of it began to collapse.

"A ghost is eating the hallway!" Gabe yelled. "MOVE!"

We stumbled into the room. The door slammed shut.

CHAPTER 12

IN THE WORKSHOP

My eyes started to adjust. Gabe was staring back at the closed door, shaking.

"Don't worry, Gabe, the ghosts seem to be room-specific. Like the one that didn't follow us into the hallway."

"Okay," Gabe said, a little uncertainly. But he turned and saw what I saw: a room that looked like the junk-filled workshop my brother Jimi had set up in our garage.

"What the heck is this place?" we said together.

There were two large wooden drafting tables in the center. In one corner, two comfy armchairs like the ones from the library were facing each other. Between them was a very old—

"Is that a record player?" I said out loud.

Gabe and I walked over to look at it. It was pretty weird-looking. It had a huge horn thingy that curved around. I think that's where the sound would have come out. The horn connected to a sharp point resting above a cylinder.

"It looks like a giant flower or a Venus flytrap," said Gabe.

"But how does it turn on?" I asked, wishing Jimi or Jo were here.

Gabe pointed to a crank on the side. "I think you turn this," he said.

I gripped it and cranked it as hard as I could. It was a little stuck, but I managed to turn it at least five times. We waited for the record player to start up. Nothing happened.

"Must be busted," I said.

Gabe nodded and looked around to see what else was in the room. "What's this?" he said.

I turned to see what he was pointing at. Next to the drafting tables sat an opened trunk—almost like a pirate's treasure chest— filled with bits of wood, metal and paper.

"And what's *this*?" he added. Now he was hovering over what looked like a dollhouse in a glass case. Dollhouses, a treasure chest . . .

"Maybe this is supposed to be a playroom?" I said.

Gabe shook his head slowly. "No, these are maquettes," he said in an odd whisper.

"Like a baby mackerel?"

"No, a maquette is a scale model."

"Scales, mackerels—fish! I mean, you have to admit this glass case does look like an aquarium."

Gabe sighed. "Not that kind of scale. A maquette is a miniature. These maquettes are for opera sets." He lifted the hinged glass front of the case.

"Charlotte must have designed and made these. Then the actual set builders would use them to make the real thing."

"I guess they didn't have Lego back then." I yawned. "You play with the toys. I'm going to see what this book is."

I pulled the book out of my backpack and gasped when I saw the cover.

"Gabe, look! Birch bark! This must be the book from that sketch."

Gabe was too obsessed with the models to answer. I heard him squeak with excitement. I couldn't wait to open the book, but I also couldn't help smiling as he puttered around the models, breaking out in song as he made the figurines dance around the tiny stages.

"I'm introducing Madama Butterfly to Rigoletto!" He was beaming. "They're friends!"

"That's nice," I said, but I wasn't too interested. Instead, the pictures and posters on the wall above the record player had caught my eye.

There were so many pictures on the walls, although these were more like technical drawings, not photos or postcards.

There was one old poster for a magic act hanging by the chairs, though, for someone called Frances the Fantastic: The Magnificent Magical Muse. But it was faded and peeling at the edges. I inched forward to get a closer look and saw—

"The woman from the photo!"

Sure enough, the woman on the poster was the same woman from the photos in the bedroom, with the same pose, her arm outstretched, wearing the same starry cape.

"Check this out!" I called to Gabe. "This is so cool!"

The woman's expression was even more impressive in the poster's illustration—the sparks from the end of her wand sprayed outward, and within them, I could make out these words: "*ENCHANTING...BEWITCHING...ENTICING! YOU WILL BE SPELLBOUND BY THE SIREN'S SONG!*"

And as I peered closer, I could see underneath what looked like the words "*FEATURING . . . CHERUBO, THE GIANT—*" But then the bottom of the poster was too damaged and old to read any more. Whatever other attractions her show had boasted were lost to time.

While Gabe continued to play with the mackerels, I sat down under the magician poster and cracked open the book.

It was a journal—or actually, more like a creator's notebook or scrapbook. Flipping through, I saw there were sketches and schematics for sets. One page had a weird drawing of what looked like piano keys with a bunch of other blueprint-looking sketches.

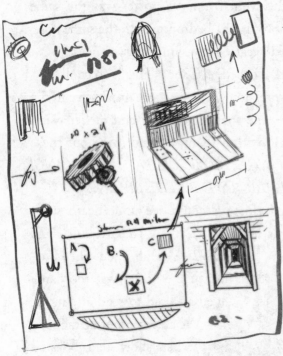

"Hey, Gabe, what the heck is this?" I held up the journal with the piano drawing.

"I'll be right with you, I'm just . . ." he trailed off, having a spacey Zed moment of his own.

I knew I wouldn't be getting his attention any time soon. I turned back to the journal and kept flipping through. There was a drawing of the horn thing, with a waxed tube and the word "gramophone" underneath. And at the very front was a selection of cast lists from a bunch of operas and performances. There were many works and roles listed, but only one name appeared in each one, although it was spelled slightly differently in some cases. Franc*i*s Deslaurier or Franc*es* Deslaurier. F.D.!

"Gabe!" I called out. "I know what 'F.D.' stands for!"

He stopped mid-aria and shrugged. "Really?"

I walked over and showed him the pages with the cast lists and the name Francis Deslaurier next to all those roles. Papageno, Cherubino, Spoletta . . .

"Not starring roles, but not small ones either," Gabe said.

I turned the page in the book to see if there were any more. I found this letter pasted there:

1901
To I.E.—

Every time I write that nickname, I have to laugh. What a silly joke we have—just for us! Out in the world, you're sometimes FrancIs; sometimes, and always to me, FrancEs. What a sea change caused by just one letter. When you're in costume, you can be Mimi from La Bohème, you're Spoletta from Tosca, you're Lensky from Eugene Onegin—i.e., often a man. Yet when it is just us, we are both women, making our way, secretly together, through this strange and obscure world. I could recognize you anywhere, spy your face in a crowd no matter what you are wearing.

But I am writing you about a serious matter, I.E. What to do about our working space? I am puzzling this out now. The sets must go somewhere, and your magic props are so numerous now that we likely need another room just for those. Perhaps we need a shared work-space? Better sightlines and a better perspective. How would I have made the Flying Dutchman disappear so well without your professional expertise? How would you have wowed the crown princes of Europe with your magic without my costumes and sense of the dramatic?

I propose we work in the same workshop. What do you say to that?

Write back soon with your thoughts.

Yours in business,
C.S.

As I held out the book and read the letter aloud, a piece of paper fell from its pages to the floor. Gabe picked it up. It was a photo of a woman in an elaborate magician's outfit, sitting on a chaise longue facing the camera. Behind her, standing, was a young Charlotte dressed in a glittering white robe. They were both smiling for the camera—something I didn't think people in old photos ever did!

I took the photo from Gabe and looked closer. And suddenly, everything clicked: I had been right, beyond a doubt. The faces in the photos we'd put on the mantel were the same person. And now I understood I.E. The singer in the costumes, sometimes dressed as a man—Francis. The magician—Frances. What had Charlotte written? *"I could recognize you anywhere, spy your face in a crowd."* I clutched the photo to my heart. Even when she didn't look like herself, I saw her.

Francis *and* Frances.

"Gabe, this is F.D. Look how happy she and Charlotte are together."

I thought of Sam and Jo. Of Lysander and Yves. I turned the photo over and saw that like so many others in Charlotte's collection, it had an inscription on the back: *"A reminder that I should never be afraid of a leap of faith. After all, I do not make that leap into the darkness alone—with your hand in mine, I feel as if nothing can touch us. Ever yours, C.S."*

"This is beautiful," I said. "Francis is also"—I pointed to the poster—"Frances the Fantastic."

"So that's why we had to have *those* five frames in that order in the other room," Gabe said. "Frances *was* in all of them."

I nodded. "The key to escaping that first room was seeing Frances in the crowd, like Charlotte did. Which is why we had to add the magician's picture and not just the pictures from the operas Charlotte worked on."

"So they met because they both worked in opera. That *is* romantic," said Gabe.

"Right, and that was the key to escaping the first room. And the key to understanding how we escaped the hallway is on the back of this photo here: the leap of faith. They took a leap of faith into the darkness together. Like we just did."

"The darkness. The unknown. Together." He furrowed his brow. "Weird, though, that they never mentioned Frances in the info package for this place."

"I think that's the point. It's something we had to discover for ourselves, using this." I tapped the birchbark cover. "That's why the ghost in that seance showed us the hidden drawing, with Charlotte holding the journal."

"You said that wasn't a ghost." Gabe's eyes darted around.

"Oh, that's right. It was gravity."

That seemed to calm him down.

But now I had chills. "Charlotte's journal is the key to everything, because now we know this isn't just some puzzle or game. I think Charlotte wants us to uncover a whole secret love story!"

"That nobody else knew about?"

"Well, they couldn't be public with it. That's why she said they were 'secretly together.' Just think about how much trouble H.K. Taylor had getting *The Monster's Castle* published with some fictional gay monsters. Charlotte and Frances were a real couple decades before Taylor was even born."

"Yeah, that can't have been easy."

"I don't know where *this* story is going," I said, "but if the first room was about them meeting and the hallway was about taking a leap of faith together, what does *this* room represent?" Then I thought back to the letter. "Charlotte wrote to Frances suggesting they work together. Maybe this is that workspace?"

Gabe pointed at the desks. "Makes sense—there are two desks, and they're facing each other."

"So they could gaze into each other's eyes as they worked!" I swooned. "See? I knew it was romantic."

"Oh, and look what I found—it wasn't just Charlotte designing the maquettes." Gabe led me over to one and lifted up a mini carpet in a mini room, revealing the letters *CF* burned into the wood.

"I wasn't sure what this was when I first saw it," he said. "But now that we know about Frances, I think it's their joint signature. Both *C* and *F* designed these sets. And if you think about it, you can see them both using their skills to make these."

"They are beautiful."

"That's thanks to Charlotte, the *C*," Gabe explained.

"And what about the *F*?"

"These don't just look cool—they are deceptive." He walked over to a framed newspaper article on the wall. The headline was "How Did They Do That?!"

"This article talks about Charlotte's set for *The Flying Dutchman*, where the ghost captain and his ship would disappear and then immediately reappear on a completely different part of the stage! No one could figure out how. Sometimes, the ghosts would even hover in the air, *over* the audience!" He shivered.

"Magic tricks," I said.

Gabe nodded. "That *was* something new in Charlotte's work, and now we know it was because she and Frances began working together."

"A true partnership! Charlotte was the engineer with the theatrical flair; Frances was the magician." I looked around with a newfound appreciation for the weird little Lego sets.

"All these models have some hidden magic tricks in them," Gabe said. "Trapdoors, passageways under the stage."

His mention of doors and passageways made me notice something about the room we were in.

"There's only one door in here—the one we came in through. Not even a bathroom or a closet."

Gabe stared at the door. "And we know that going back through it means getting kicked out. So there must be an exit hidden in here too. But where is it?"

"And what do we need to do to find it?"

"Anything else useful in the book?"

I scanned quickly over the next few pages. No letters, but a lot of sketches of gears and pulleys and stuff.

"Hey, these look like the drawings on the walls." I pointed to all the sketches hanging above us.

On closer inspection, those sketches turned out to be blueprints, and they matched the models in the glass cases.

Gabe kept looking from the blueprints to the maquettes and back again, then he chuckled and pointed to the treasure chest.

"What's so funny?" I asked.

"Lego."

"Lego?"

"Earlier you were joking. But didn't you ever do those Lego sets where you had to build something based on plans in a booklet?"

"I tended to do my own bespoke designs."

"Well, the blueprints on the walls are like those booklets, and that"—he pointed at the chest—"is a huge box full of Lego."

I was impressed. "Good eye, my clever friend."

Gabe bowed. "Thank you."

"Okay, so what you're saying is that we need to use these parts, following one of these blueprints, to recreate one of these maquettes?"

Gabe nodded. "Yup, I think that's the idea."

"Then I have just one more question: Which model are we supposed to build?"

CHAPTER 13

A WORKSPACE FOR TWO

Gabe and I spent a good half an hour arguing about which "room" was the right one to build. I said it had to be the biggest one, which turned out to be for *Aida*, because "it would be the most complicated and therefore the hardest one to do."

Sound logic, or so I thought.

"But *Aida* is tragedy," Gabe said. "I think to reflect the early days of their relationship, Charlotte would have chosen a romance or a comedy."

"I knew you were an incurable romantic! Then which one is it?"

"The middle one." Gabe pointed at a colorful maquette. It wasn't the biggest or the smallest, but it was golden with red curtains. "The one from *The Marriage of Figaro*. The only comedy here."

"*Rigoletto* and *Madama Butterfly* don't come with a laugh track?"

"More like a funeral dirge. But the cast lists you showed me tell us that in *The Marriage of Figaro*, Frances sang the part of Cherubino, which is often sung by a woman dressed as a man."

"Very cool!" I said, raising my arms in a cheer. Then I refocused. "Okay, following along so far."

"It's a comedy where everybody is trying to rip the lovers apart. But they come together at the end."

"Spoiler alert!"

"You've seen it. With me."

I had a sudden but vague memory of something like the opera Gabe was describing, but then I remembered falling asleep and dreaming about knitting a sweater out of spaghetti.

"You can't expect me to remember *all* the plot details," I said defensively. "It's not like *The Screaming Skull at Skeleton Rock*. Love that book. Now that's *real* drama."

Gabe shook his head sadly. "Anyway, there are a bunch of reasons to think that *The Marriage of Figaro* is the one we need to recreate."

"Okay, I'm sold." I looked at the pile of pieces and the ornate model under glass. "But this is going to take forever."

"Then we'd better get started." Gabe said. We got to work.

Building an exact replica of an already tiny set with tiny pieces is like trying to do a jigsaw puzzle made of rice. It would strain my already low patience threshold to list how many times I had to find some little matchstick-sized piece at the bottom of the chest and hand it to Gabe (who was having way too much fun), but let's just say it was *a lot*.

Plus, I had to sift through tons of extra pieces—tables, chairs, curtains and framed paintings—that didn't seem to match any of the models. I threw those back into the chest.

Finally, after at least two hours, we stood back and admired our handiwork. "It looks just like the original," I said. "Right down to the funky piano in the corner."

"That's a harpsichord."

"You made that word up."

Gabe growled.

So did my stomach. "So now that we have built up an appetite *and* destroyed our eyesight finding all these little pieces, what do we do with the model?"

"I was hoping it would just spring a trapdoor or something," Gabe said. "But maybe it's like the photos on the mantel and we need to put it somewhere?"

We tried putting it on the drafting tables, but nothing happened. We used a couple of chairs to carefully lift the model on top of each glass case. Nothing. As we lifted it down, I slipped and tiny bits fell out and skidded across the floor. I was getting frustrated and just wanted to throw the whole thing against the wall.

"I'm stumped," said Gabe, carefully picking up the harpsichord and putting it back in place.

Something about his tone of voice calmed my nerves. I was glad I wasn't here alone. I wouldn't have had the patience.

A couple of other pieces had come to rest against the chest. I walked over to pick them up, and for some reason—almost like something was controlling my hand—I closed the lid. It clicked shut.

"Hey, Gabe?"

"Yeah?" He looked over.

I pointed at the lid, where a . . . um, let's say maquette-sized square of wood was carved into the top.

He smiled. "Let's go!"

We carefully put all the loose pieces back in place, then rested the model on the lid. It fit perfectly.

There was a click and a whir from somewhere under the floor.

"YES!" We jumped and gave each other a high five.

When we landed back on our feet, we must have jiggled something in the old record player because it sprung to life. The strains of a song came out through the giant horn.

"Hey, I recognize this! It's the Charleston!" I said, starting to swing my arms and legs in time with the music.

"Let me guess," said Gabe, sighing. "You know all the moves."

"Heck yeah! My mom always plays old dance music like this. You know that!"

I kept moving, holding my arms out and kicking my legs side to side, then crossing them in front. Gabe laughed and tried to join, watching me and following the steps.

"This is so great! I *knew* Charlotte knew how to party!"

Suddenly, the music stopped. We could still hear the needle on the record—a scratchy, repetitive tone. Then we could hear a tinny voice. It sounded far away and was partly obscured by an ocean of static.

"Please tell me that's not a ghost!" Gabe said, at the exact same time as I said, "MORE GHOSTS PLEASE!"

"*Zed . . . and Gabe . . .*" said the record player.

Gabe screamed, looking around in panic. "It knows our names?!"

The temperature dropped again. "*. . . you look but do not see . . .*"

The chest beside us began to shake. The lid opened like a shot, jettisoning our model like a catapult. The model hit the door and smashed into a gazillion pieces.

Gabe groaned and fell to his knees. "I was sure that was the right one."

The ghostly voice continued, "*If you do not leave now . . . you will never . . . leave . . . this house . . .*"

The door opened, revealing the hallway, now repaired and fully lit! The voice began counting down. "*Five . . . four . . .*"

"LET'S GO!" screeched Gabe, springing up and heading for the door.

I looked from the hallway back to the workroom. Something wasn't right.

"*Three . . . two . . .*"

"No! It's a test!" I said. "Charlotte *wants* us to figure this out, no matter how scared we get!"

"*One . . .*"

"Encore!" I yelled, and Gabe stopped.

The door slammed shut, and even I jumped. The record was silent for a moment more, then continued, "*You have . . . one . . . final . . . chance.*" The voice faded into silence. For a moment, we stood completely still, not even breathing for fear of angering any ghosts. Then the record started playing the Charleston again, like nothing had happened.

"We should have escaped," said Gabe. He looked distraught, and his eyes kept darting around the room as if he expected a new terror at any moment.

What if I had unfairly given him an encore? He could have left, but he stayed. With me. My eyes welled with tears. I walked over to where he stood and hugged him. He stopped shaking and hugged me back. After a long moment, we stepped apart.

"I guess we gotta go back to the drawing board," I said. "Thanks for staying."

Gabe started to nod, then stopped. He looked thoughtful. "Hey, maybe that's it."

"That's what?"

"The drawing board." He got up and walked over to the opened chest, keeping an eye on the record player. He leaned over the side of the chest and soon popped back up, holding a small desk.

"Look familiar?" he asked.

I looked closer and nodded. "It's like the two over there." I pointed to the drafting tables.

"Yup. This wasn't an extra piece. It's not from any opera set. It's part of the room Charlotte actually wanted us to see—and to build. The one that really meant the most to her."

"This one," I said. "So all these fancy-schmancy sets and blueprints are misdirections?"

"I think so. Designed to make someone think this room is about Charlotte's career. Just like we thought we needed career photos for the mantelpiece."

"But the book keeps telling us this whole house is revealing a story about the two of them."

Gabe nodded. "And we fell for the trick *again*."

"The good news is that we're still in the game."

"For now. We don't know how many more rooms we have to get out of. And this one took us *way* too long."

My plan of solving the mystery quickly and making it out in time for Halloween was falling apart.

"Well," Gabe said, "as my dad and Sam are always telling me, the best time to start a job is yesterday. The second best is right now."

I nodded. "You heard the ghost—we get one more try, so let's get to work." I looked around. "But how do we assemble this room without a blueprint?"

"The room we're in *is* the blueprint," Gabe said.

"That's really sweet, actually," I said. "No need for a lot of decoration or ostentation—just a simple place where they could work together quietly."

After an hour or so, we had assembled an exact replica of the workroom. Right down to a mini gramophone, which, despite my repeated attempts, refused to talk to me.

"Ready?" Gabe said.

I nodded, and we carefully lifted the model onto the chest, then held our breath.

There was more whirring and clicking, and then the door started to open.

The same door we'd used to enter the room.

"Oh no! We got it wrong again."

"We're going home!" I wanted to cry.

But something was different. Instead of leading back to the hallway, the door had opened onto the landing of the grand staircase.

And standing in the middle of the open doorway was a ghostly pale girl in a flapper dress, holding a crowbar.

CHAPTER 14

HYACINTH THE GHOST

"For the last time, I am not a ghost!"

"Exactly what a ghost would say!" I said.

"WHY WOULD A GHOST LIE?" howled the ghost, who had introduced herself as Hyacinth.

"Why WOULDN'T a ghost lie?" I thought this was a good point, but Hyacinth moaned and put her head in her hands.

"Look, I'm not a ghost. I work here."

"So do the ghosts."

Really, I felt like I was winning this debate hands down. I mean, the evidence was clear: ghostly complexion, old-timey dress, old-timey haircut, flapper headband, looked like she was thirteen but was probably one hundred and three. She was a good head shorter than Gabe, and everyone knows that people in the olden times were small. I didn't know how the crowbar fit into my theory, but ghosts do weird stuff all the time.

"Say boo," I said.

"No. I work here with my mom. Bertie? The groundskeeper you met yesterday?"

"She's a ghost too???!!!!"

Gabe decided it was time to step in. "Hey, Hyacinth, maybe let Zed fist-bump you."

"I've always wanted to fist-bump a ghost!"

She sighed. "Seriously?"

Gabe nodded. "Or we can just keep arguing."

She rolled her eyes. "FINE."

Hyacinth leaned her pale arm toward me, and I prepared for the cold touch of the undead. I reached over and fist-bumped her outstretched hand.

Warm and alive.

"Rats," I said. "So if you're NOT a ghost, why did you suddenly appear and magically move the doorway?"

"I didn't move the doorway."

"Then a ghost must have!" I was back on track.

"No, no, no. Well, maybe in a way. Charlotte did it."

An almost imperceptible breeze mussed my hair.

"Charlotte? You mean she's still here, working behind the scenes?"

Hyacinth rolled her eyes. "Uh . . . no. Kind of. She left

meticulous instructions on how to maintain everything, but we never see what's actually going on."

"The ghost in the machine! Literally," I joked.

"But what does that mean?" asked Gabe.

"It means we have places where we add lubricating oil a few times a year, and some pipes that need to be turned on and off. Stuff like that. But never the full picture. I've only ever been in a couple of the rooms myself—and Bertie's been in only a few more than that."

"Okay, well, what are the pipes for?" Gabe asked.

Hyacinth shrugged. "Don't know. No one has ever found a challenge where there's water. But the room you were in is cool. It turns slowly—too slowly for you to notice while you're inside. And it somehow knows if you got the answer right or not."

"The ghost in the gramophone knows," I said.

"The what now?"

"Never mind," said Gabe quickly. "But did we get it right?"

"Yup. That's why I'm here—to get you for dinner instead of sending you home."

"Dinner?"

"Right down those stairs." She pointed. "Bertie has laid out a top-notch spread."

I sniffed the air like a shaggy dog and made out

the unmistakable aroma of breakfast for dinner. Bacon, eggs, toast, baked beans. I licked my lips. We hadn't eaten all day, and I was famished.

"Time to make a mad dash for the hash and mash!" I slid down the banister while Hyacinth and Gabe walked down like a couple of rubes. I dismounted with a perfect two-footed backward landing on the marble floor, then I heard a crack and looked down. The tile I was standing on had snapped in half.

"I thought marble flooring would be a little tougher," I said. "Sorry."

"It's not real marble," Hyacinth said. "It's painted to look like marble. It's linoleum, but it's gotten brittle over the years." She lifted the crowbar and pointed to the door Bertie had shown us before. "Dinner's in there."

We made our way into the dining room.

"Why do you have that crowbar?" Gabe asked.

"I was wondering that too!" I interjected.

Hyacinth let out a deep sigh and deflated a little, like a leaking balloon. "This whole place is starting to break down. I don't think Charlotte expected the scavenger hunt to take quite so long. I needed the crowbar because your door didn't open all the way and I had to give it a little help. To be fair, you're only the third team to make it past that room."

"She was too good for her own good," Gabe said.

"And the flapper dress is your work uniform?" I joked.

"Yeah, do you like it?" She moved from side to side, and

the fabric swayed with her. "It's very old. But it's so comfortable. I wear it because there's a room off the main foyer with a series of bells and alarms. If this one specific alarm goes off, I go stand in a closet and wave my arms wearing this amazing uniform."

"I like it. It has the Zed stamp of approval."

She bowed her head. "Thank you."

"Wait, closet?" asked Gabe. "Do you jump out and scare someone? Like at a carnival haunted house?"

She shook her head. "Nope. Weirder than that. I'm alone the whole time. The instructions say that if this specific alarm goes off, I have to stand on a particular spot and act all scary and stuff. A light turns on and shines like a spotlight. But why is there a spotlight in a room like that? No idea. Bertie used to have to do the same job when she was a kid."

"Shouldn't you be waiting in case the alarm goes off now?" I stuffed a scone into my mouth.

"No need. It got triggered a couple of hours ago, right

before that couple left. I was only helping with the crowbar because Bertie was getting the food ready."

I stuffed a blueberry muffin into my mouth and looked around. We were alone in the dining room.

I swallowed. "Wait! Dean and Soraya LEFT?"

"I'd almost forgotten they were here," Gabe said.

"I kind of liked her," I said. "But I'm not surprised she got too scared."

Hyacinth shrugged. "All I know is that when I came out of the closet, they were running down the stairway. She was crying and yelling something about a real-life poltergeist, and not wanting to lose her hair color. He was running after her but stopped to yell at Bertie that he didn't believe the treasure was even here, and that he thought the whole trip was a waste of his 'valuable time.' His words, not mine."

"I get that," Gabe said. "The 'too scared' part."

"I don't," I said. "I mean, we've seen some ghosts, but nothing too scary. And I keep hoping Frances will show up so we can get some answers."

"Frances?" Hyacinth seemed genuinely confused.

"Frances. Charlotte's *friend*."

Hyacinth cocked an eyebrow. "Why did you say 'friend' like that?"

I piled some bacon on my plate and wondered if I should say anything more, but as I was doing that, Gabe blurted out the whole story—or at least what we'd gleaned from the journal and the three puzzles we'd solved so far.

". . . and so we think the whole house and the treasure hunt are about their love for each other," he finished.

Hyacinth's eyes grew wide. "This is making a lot of stuff make a lot of sense."

"Like what?" asked Gabe.

She opened her mouth, then closed it. She furrowed her brow. She seemed to be thinking about something.

"Listen," I said, "you said we were one of the few teams to make it this far. If you have info that could help us, please share it."

Gabe nodded. "We just want to get to the bottom of this mystery."

"Hmmm. Well, since you told me about Frances, I think I can tell you why Charlotte set up this challenge in the first place."

We leaned in close.

CHAPTER 15

HYACINTH'S STORY

"Like my mom said, Charlotte never married or had kids. Bertie and I are descendants of Charlotte's brother, Xavier. And just like this crowbar, he was a bit of a tool."

"I'll have to remember that line," I said. "But how so?"

She shook her head. "A bunch of reasons. For one, he never took Charlotte's work seriously. He burned a lot of her letters when she died, but enough survived to give a glimpse of their relationship. He does not come off well. He was always running her down for her work. He said she should be a homemaker, not a set-maker."

"Sounds like a bit of a jerk," Gabe said, and I nodded agreement.

"And now that you've told me about Frances, some other stuff makes sense. Like how Xavier once wrote 'Now that she's gone, I will inherit it all.' We never knew what he meant and why he was so sure. He wrote that *years* before Charlotte died and she'd stopped going anywhere."

"You think he might have meant 'Now that Frances has left'?" asked Gabe.

I felt my skin tingle. "Wait, left for where? They broke up?! They seemed so happy, though." I couldn't believe Charlotte's story would lead to heartbreak like this.

"Well, there was no way Charlotte and Frances could have gotten married back then. So maybe he meant, like, legally he would get all of Charlotte's money?" suggested Gabe.

"They couldn't get legally married, it's true," I said. "But they were together as much as any couple could be. We know it."

Gabe handed Hyacinth the picture of the smiling Frances and Charlotte.

She ran a finger gently over their faces. "That's so lovely. Posing like a bride and bride. Xavier did mention from time to time that Charlotte had a friend who would also die a spinster."

I chuckled. "Spinsters! I've read about relationships like this in lots of old books. Two women who live together, never marrying, but are clearly close. Those who needed to get it would get it: they were a couple. But they wouldn't seem gay to someone who wasn't paying close attention. It was a way to validate the relationships of people who chose to live together."

"Well, Xavier was also no fan of what he called Charlotte's 'bohemian lifestyle.' He said she was consorting with 'an evil magician' who he wished would '*truly* disappear,' and we never knew what *that* meant either. But once he wrote that he was so disgusted, he wouldn't visit for holidays or birthdays."

I scratched my head, thinking. "You said he burned a lot of Charlotte's letters. She must have suspected he'd try to do something like that, so she preserved some here in this book." I tapped the birchbark cover.

Gabe took back the picture and I slid it into the journal. "He was no fan of Charlotte's, and he hated Frances enough to want her to disappear. So why are his descendants still here?" Gabe asked.

"The curse," Hyacinth said in a whisper.

"The curse?!"

"Charlotte started getting famous. Which meant she started getting rich. Guess who started hanging around a bit more?"

"Xavier."

"He joked that he was just making sure she wasn't squandering *his* fortune. He said he had to keep her from scandal so the money would continue rolling in."

"What a charmer," I said.

"Yeah, I'm not proud that he's the one I'm descended

from. But when she shut herself away and started building this place, she didn't let him visit anymore. He'd watch the different parts of the building go up and get angry about the cost. We have some letters he wrote to her lawyers about it. It's possible he was the one spreading all the rumors about her being a witch and losing her mind."

"Maybe he was hoping someone would lock her up and stop the building?"

She nodded. "Then when she was dying, she summoned Xavier to her side. I imagine him happily rubbing his hands together, anticipating the fortune she was about to leave him."

"But she didn't?"

"No, she did. Sort of. This is where the curse comes in. Her will stipulated that he and his descendants were the sole heirs of Glyndebourne Manor, the grounds and everything in it."

"So then why are we here?"

"There was a catch. The manor was to remain closed for a decade after her death. Then, and only then, would Xavier be allowed to, in her words, 'lead a search for the treasure.'"

"Search?" I asked.

"Treasure?" asked Gabe.

"I think she knew Xavier would never agree to share anything. So the will said he couldn't search himself but only help others look. And Charlotte said the only way to find it would be to finally see the world through her eyes."

"Bet Xavier loved that," Gabe and I joked.

"He had no choice. She said that if he tried to break in, the house would burn and he'd lose it all. Then she breathed her last breath. Her final words were gibberish—or so we thought. Just two letters: *I* and *E*. And now we know what that means."

All three of us exchanged a look.

"Frances."

The wind howled outside.

"Despite the warning," Hyacinth continued, "Xavier still tried to break in. He took an axe to the front door, but it only *looked* like wood. In fact, the door was metal. He had to wear a cast on his wrists for a few months to recover. I think that made him take the curse a little more seriously, so he bided his time."

"Stewing."

"For sure. On the tenth anniversary of her death, the house mysteriously opened, as if by a hidden hand."

The wind whistled. Okay, this time it was just me doing sound effects. Gabe swung his leg at me under the table.

"Xavier ran into the front hall, expecting to be greeted with, I dunno, piles of cash and jewels laid out on the floor. Or maybe even a safe or something he could crack."

Gabe and I were leaning in close, hanging on every word.

"Instead, on this very table"—she tapped the dining table emphatically—"was a leather-bound book with a series of handwritten instructions. The ones we've been following ever since. And the keys to a series of passageways inside the walls."

"But no treasure?"

She shook her head. "Nowhere to be found. The passageways lead to the secret places where we do the maintenance stuff."

"But he was inside the house now, so why not just tear the place apart?" Gabe asked.

"Well, he tried. Xavier was so mad he pulled books off the shelves, looking for some hidden safe. But the floor opened up, and he was dumped into the wine cellar. It was empty. He rushed up the cellar stairs, which led outside, and found the front door locked again. He couldn't get back inside."

"For how long?"

"A week, as it turned out. Xavier spent that time digging up almost every inch of the property, but he never found anything. He was chopping up a birch tree on the grounds out front when the door swung open again. This time, he sheepishly went in and finally grabbed the instruction book."

She sipped some tea. "When he started following those instructions, only then did the house begin to—I'm not sure how else to describe it—cooperate. But he clearly missed something because he died bitter, frustrated and treasureless. So for generations, we've worked here, keeping the place running and hoping someone will help us solve the mystery."

"Amazing," Gabe and I said in unison.

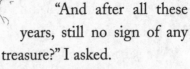

"And after all these years, still no sign of any treasure?" I asked.

"Nope. There was a bit of hoopla at the beginning—I think about a hundred people volunteered to help Xavier by staying two nights. But all of them ran out of time before they figured out what Charlotte wanted them to look for."

"It *is* tricky," I said.

"And the longer this search has gone on, the more the world has looked away, and we've kind of become a quirky ghost story, if that. My grandmother, the one in the video, didn't like this place any more than Xavier did. But she tried to at least make it a kind of touristy haunted house attraction. That worked for a while, but this year, we only had that one couple sign up. That's why Bertie called the radio station after hearing your interview."

"The mysterious caller was your mom?" Gabe exclaimed at the same time as I yelled, "It was Bertie!"

"Who else? She thought, why not? Two kid detectives who wanted to see ghosts?"

Gabe held up a finger. "One kid detective who wanted to see that." He pointed the finger at me.

"Well, Bertie and I kind of love this old shack, so she thought it was worth a try."

We sat for a while, taking this all in and munching on some seriously good butter tarts. That means no raisins, BTW.

"Well, Hyacinth, in that interview, we *also* said we wanted a mystery with ice cream," I said.

"Sorry to disappoint," she said. "There is a refrigeration unit we have to maintain but no freezer—ergo, no ice cream."

"Latin," Gabe whispered to himself, and he smiled.

I sighed wistfully and picked up another butter tart. "No ice cream? Tragedy."

"Charlotte sounds like she was kind of awesome," said Gabe. "I wish I'd known her."

"And I wish we'd known Frances too," I said.

"Yeah, finding out about Frances just kinda makes me like this place even more. I wonder if she and Charlotte would be happy with how Bertie and I have taken care of it"—she smiled—"since this is probably the last chance to find the treasure."

"*Last* chance?" I asked.

Hyacinth tapped the crowbar, which was leaning against her chair. "Bertie says it won't be safe to visit in another five years, let alone twenty-five. Repairs cost money, and with no treasure, there's no future."

"Do you think there *is* a treasure?"

"Charlotte was super famous . . . like a celebrity. She was also *really* rich. And she wouldn't put people through this just for kicks. That wasn't her style. I do think she wanted to reward someone who could solve the mystery, see through the puzzles. See Frances. Someone who could commune with the spirits and understand their love story. Plus I can feel it. Something is hidden here. Something *big*."

I looked at Gabe and winked. He winked back. The gears in our heads were turning.

"We have an idea," I said.

Gabe nodded. "We could team up. We help your family solve the mystery before it's too late, and we get some of the treasure to pay for the raddest wedding in the history of weddings."

"So, ghost girl, whaddya say? Are we a team? Want to bring an end to the family curse?"

Hyacinth sat silently for a long time while Gabe and I chowed down on some delicious currant buns.

"Come on," I said, nudging her elbow.

Finally, she smiled. "I need to be honest: I don't know much more than you guys do—and in some cases, less—but I do have this notebook with some instructions. What the heck, let's do it."

"Whoop!" Gabe and I cheered and hugged our new pal.

I gave her an extra-long hug, just to be sure she wasn't, in fact, a ghost.

"You're crushing me!"

"Rats."

I let her go. "So, ghost girl . . . what next?"

CHAPTER 16

THE MUSIC ROOM

Hyacinth opened her instruction book. "According to these notes, I'm supposed to prep the room you're going to next, and then Bertie was going to take you there after you had eaten." She tapped her finger on her chin. "But I think we can just go there now, and you can help with the tasks."

"Excelsior!" I agreed, pointing up to the ceiling.

"But won't Bertie come looking for us?" asked Gabe. We glanced around.

"Well, I came to grab you from the workshop because she was busy with some floor repair. The yelling guy who left stamped too hard on the back staircase. I'll leave her a note," said Hyacinth.

Gabe pulled his notepad and a pen from a pocket in his pants. She raised her eyebrows.

"Too bad this dress doesn't have pockets," she noted. "Those pants look really useful." She took the notepad and scribbled something, then ripped out the piece of paper and put it on an empty plate in the middle of the table.

We all stood up.

"Okay, so where to exactly?" Gabe asked.

She consulted the book again. "A room on the fourth floor."

"Take us there!" I said.

We left the dining room and went through the passage to the grand staircase again.

"Did you really say *fourth floor*?" I asked. "This haunted house has too many stairs and too few ghosts."

Gabe smiled. "I like it better that way."

She took us to a room at the front of the house, behind a door with a musical note on it. (Hyacinth had the musical note key with her.)

"Since I told Bertie I'd stick with you guys, I kept the keys. I don't want to miss *anything* else, and you two nerds are going to help me find out all I can about Aunt Charlotte. *Et voilà*."

She opened the door, and we were greeted by a small and cozy room with two huge windows. Light streamed in, and I was grateful for it. For such a huge house, there were weirdly few windows. I didn't know how someone could live here and not feel sad. The "sun" room we slept in didn't even have any sun!

The wallpaper here in the music room was covered in pink and white peonies, with birds flitting around a giant foun-

tain, and the floor was carpeted. It was still a beautiful moss-like green. Under the windows was a large fainting couch. In the corner was a small dusty piano with a clay vase on top. Hyacinth pointed to it. "I have to go do something with that piano." Against the opposite wall was a wooden cabinet.

While Hyacinth fiddled with the piano, I looked out one of the windows. I had been right about the orientation of the manor the previous night in the library—the house faced north. It was disorienting to walk through the house, but it was nice to feel grounded again. The window looked out over the gravel drive—no cars. Dean and Soraya were definitely gone.

It was golden hour, and everything was coated in a beautiful glow, like Willoughby when I put new batteries in him. The scene was so calm—things left untouched by human hands for who knew how many years. It looked like a painting.

The leaves from the trees were almost all on the ground, yellow and orange and red, just like the colors of the sun across the sky. I pictured kids getting ready for tomorrow, making sure their costumes fit, planning their routes. My mom would have gotten the maps printed by now.

And I wouldn't be there to see it. I wiped a tear from my eye and sniffled.

Gabe patted my shoulder. "Now that there are three of us, I bet we'll be home in time for trick-or-treating, Zed."

"All the good candy will be gone," I said, sighing.

"More candy corn for me!" Gabe replied.

I made a face and was about to criticize his taste yet again when we heard a loud crash behind us. I whirled around.

Hyacinth was standing with a guilty look on her face, her

hands in front of her as if she were holding something. The remains of the clay vase littered the green carpet at her feet.

"Oops," she said, looking from her hands to the mess below in dismay.

"What did you *do*?" Gabe looked around frantically and made for the door. "The spirits are gonna get us!"

I followed him, tugging his sleeve. "Gabe, relax. Nothing's gonna—"

Behind us, I heard the sound of a piano.

"Hyacinth, that won't help Gabe cal—" I turned around.

Hyacinth was still standing where she'd dropped the vase, frozen. She wasn't touching the piano. It was playing on its own!

"Whoa!" I said, surprised.

Hyacinth snapped out of her trance. "How the heck is it doing that?!" she said, pointing at the piano.

"Could it be Bertie controlling the keys remotely?" I asked.

The piano played on, a simple but deliciously creepy tune.

"No," said Hyacinth, shaking her head, "there was nothing in the instructions about playing the piano from another room."

Gabe jumped and let go of the doorknob, clutched at my sleeve, then squeezed my upper arm.

"I'm going to have permanent nail marks in my skin if you keep doing this," I said.

The piano continued to play.

"I was hoping we were done with ghosts," he said.

Hyacinth's eyes widened. "This has happened to you *before*? And you're still here?" She rushed at us, her hand outstretched, ready to grab the doorknob and turn the handle—

"NO!" I yelled. I pressed my back flat against the door and put my hands out.

She flinched. "Zed, this is freaking me out!"

"STOP! You can't go through the door, or we have to *leave the competition*!"

She froze.

Gabe let go of my sleeve. "Competition? Zed, it's just us! Why *are* we still here?"

I inhaled and lowered my arms. "Let's all take a deep breath. We're here to help Sam and Jo. We've come this far. Don't you want to know how it all ends? With Charlotte and Frances?"

Gabe sighed. "Yeah. I do. Encore."

Hyacinth still had her hand out to grab at the doorknob. "I don't know what you guys are talking about," she said.

"It's our special code word," I said.

She finally put her outstretched hand down. "Code word?"

I explained about the deal Gabe and I had. She thought about it, then she took a step back into the room.

"Okay. I'm in too. Encore."

"Group hug!" I said, and we piled together.

Suddenly, the piano stopped. Uh-oh, I thought. I had just convinced them both to stay and now some new creepy thing was about to happen? I hoped the hug would make them feel less afraid. I held my breath, waiting for the scare.

But nothing happened—no ghostly apparitions, no freezing cold, no darkness.

"Maybe the piano is just broken."

I walked over to examine it. There was no sheet music on it. I plunked a few keys, but it just sounded like an ordinary piano.

"You said you were supposed to check on it," I said to Hyacinth. "Is it something mechanical? Or maybe there's a tiny mouse inside, jumping on the keys out of sight?"

She joined me next to the piano. "I don't see a switch anywhere, though."

I played a few more notes. "It's normal now, see?" I said to Gabe. "Not scary."

He started to rock up and down on the balls of his feet. "So not haunted?"

"Well, I don't think that was a ghost—as much as it pains me to admit it." I turned back to Hyacinth, who was walking around the piano, inspecting it. "What do your instructions actually say?" I asked.

She took out her notebook and shook her head. "Honestly, I'm not sure. They're kind of confusing."

She showed us the page labeled with the same music note symbol as the one on the door. It was covered in scribbles and had a strange diagram of piano keys and what looked like tubes, wires and gears. The next page had a bunch of dots in vertical lines up and down the page.

I pointed to the gear and the tubes. "Gabe, is this supposed to be the piano and its insides? And what's with these scribbled dots?"

Gabe looked at the diagram. "No, that's not what a piano looks like. Whatever this is clearly has some kind of mechanism"—he pointed to the gears—"and I don't understand this illustration of the keys."

Something pinged in my memory. I racked my brains. "Wait a minute, Gabe. I saw something in the journal that looked like this earlier! When we were in the workshop. I asked you for an explanation, but you were too busy playing with those weird Legos to pay attention."

"Building the maquettes and getting us out of that room, you mean?"

"Well, technically, *I* got you out of the room," said Hyacinth. She studied her instruction book again and tapped her finger on the page with the scribbled dots. "I still don't get what I'm supposed to do in this room," she said. "These dots kind of look like Morse code. Maybe I need to decode it to get the instructions?"

"You know Morse code?" I asked, turning to her. "Like, for fun?"

"For fun, I play *Minecraft*. But in this family"—she shrugged—"taking care of an old house, in an area with spotty cell service, Bertie taught me Morse code so that if we ever had an issue, I could talk to her by blinking a flashlight." She looked at the page. "But if this is Morse code, it doesn't say anything. It's just gibberish. You said you saw something like this in the journal? Can I see?"

I took out the journal and flipped through it. "Yeah, I saw a funky-looking scribble that sort of looked like piano keys, but I—wait! Found it!"

I held up the book. Charlotte had drawn a diagram of piano keys. It was like Hyacinth's but with less detail. I turned

the page, looking for an explanation, and saw a longer handwritten entry. I read it out loud:

December 1905—Buffalo, New York. After F's birthday dinner, she asked to see the night market. She walked more quickly than I, and I rushed to keep up with her—she was trying to lead me somewhere specific. "What are you up to this time?" I asked her. She brushed those thick curls out of her face. "You'll see," she said. We soon stopped in front of a large stall with a red-and-yellow-striped awning, like a circus tent. It was filled to bursting with some of the most gaudy and grotesque trinkets I had ever seen. A panoply of caged birds and occult cards, all crowded together so that I found myself craning my neck to see everything. F took my hand and led me to an accordion player wearing a ridiculous hat with a peacock feather on it. "We'd like to see your piano," she said. He set down the accordion and beckoned us to follow him to a curtain in the back of the tent. He drew it aside and showed us what she had wanted to see: the piano. The keys were moving on their own, as if ghostly hands were playing the haunting melody.

I laughed. "Frances, it's a trifle. A cheap trick."

And then she turned to me, her eyes shining, and said something I'll never forget:

"Charlotte, there is no such thing."

What a beautiful way to live. She loved those trifles. She loved those small, silly things. Every kind of magic was equal in her eyes. Nothing was cheap, so long as it gave someone joy. What an I.E. thing to say. How exquisitely her.

I bought the pianola for her as a birthday gift and showed her its mechanism—a cylinder fitted into the top of the instrument, made of paper, punched with tiny holes that allow the pianola to "read" the notes on the sheet music, its keys pressing down through a system of pneumatic pressure tubes. Knowing how the trick happens will never ruin her experience of the magic of the pianola. And that is how I know I'll love her always. For our anniversary, I am composing a song. It doesn't have a title yet, but it will be simple and I hope it will bring her joy, even if it can't compare to the works of the masters that we both know so well.

CHAPTER 17

THE PIANOLA

"Wow," said Gabe the romantic, his hand to his chest. No one listens to that much opera without caring even a little bit about the workings of the human heart. "Not a ghost after all."

"You were right," sighed Hyacinth. "Aunt Charlotte was so cool." Then she looked back at the piano. "So to leave the room, maybe we have to play something on the piano? And then that will unlock a hidden door?"

"Makes sense," said Gabe. "But what do we play?" We walked to the piano, and he opened the lid. "There *is* a motor in here."

Hyacinth peered in. "There's one on this side too." She gestured inside the piano on the opposite end.

"What's that in the middle?" I pointed to a roll of paper wound around a metal bar. It rested in the middle of the guts of the piano, right behind the keys.

"Maybe we can get a closer look," Gabe said. "When we tune our piano, the front part comes off. There are hinges."

We all looked around, and sure enough, there were latches at the top of the piano on either end of the front panel. The panel opened forward, over the keys. We were able to look more closely at the scroll. It looked like a paper towel roll fed between two rubber rollers.

"Can we take it out?" I asked.

Gabe touched the scroll with his hands. "I think we can, but I don't want to just pull it out. That could rip it. I think it's like an old film camera. You need to wind it backward."

"These words mean very little to me," I said, "but work your magic."

He found knobs on the ends of the rollers and turned them so that the paper rewound until it wasn't between the rubber anymore. Then he gently lifted the entire scroll up and out of the piano, leaving an empty socket behind.

We examined the paper. It had a bunch of holes punched through it, cascading down its entire length. To my surprise, I recognized it instantly.

"Does this pattern look familiar to you?" I asked Hyacinth, smiling.

She peered at it more closely. "Yes!" She pulled out her book again and compared the scribbled dots to the holes on the piano roll. "It's totally the same. Not Morse code after all!"

"But what does it mean?" I asked, studying the two side by side.

"I think this paper gets fed through the machine, and the piano somehow plays it," said Gabe. "It's like robotic sheet music."

"Okay, so if Hyacinth is right and Charlotte wants us to play something on this piano, maybe we need to learn from this sheet music. Maybe we need to copy it?"

"Oh, maybe," said Gabe. "Who wants to try it?"

"That's on you, maestro," I said. "I've got butterfingers."

"That's from all those butter tarts," said Hyacinth archly. I laughed.

Gabe frowned. "I don't think I remember the whole song. Can we get it to play again?"

"Yeah, here we go," I said, replacing the scroll in the lid.

Then Gabe and I lifted the front panel and latched it back in place. He sat down at the keys. Hyacinth and I stepped back to give him space. We waited.

"Nothing's happening. Do we know how to actually get it to play?" asked Gabe.

Hyacinth studied her book. "Okay, now that we know what we are looking at, I think I understand what these instructions are saying. It says something about airflow, which is like what Aunt Charlotte said about 'a system of pneumatic tubes.' Bertie taught me that just means 'air-powered,' so that makes sense. Check the air in the tubes. Got it."

"Okay, but how?" I asked.

"Hang on, I'm still reading." She squinted at the book and brought the instructions close to her face until the paper

almost touched her nose. Then she smiled. "Okay, this is really cool."

"Did you figure it out?!"

"I think so. It says that you need to get air into the machine through the bellows, which is basically like an air pump. And you do that by pressing on the piano pedals with your foot. Try a test," she said to Gabe. "You need to pump the bellows with your feet, one on each pedal."

He pumped the pedals a few times. I heard a sound like a bike tire being inflated.

"It definitely sounds right," I said.

After a minute, Gabe stopped, huffing. "That's more work than it looks!" he said.

The piano still didn't play.

"Man!" Hyacinth threw up her arms in frustration, took a step and stomped her foot, not noticing she was about to step on the remains of the broken vase.

"Careful," I said, but she didn't hear me, because at that moment, the piano started to play.

Gabe sat and watched the keys press and depress on their own, playing a simple little melody with only a few notes. It ended.

"Okay, I've got it," he said. He repeated the melody perfectly, using both hands to play the two octaves. He finished with a big grin.

"Nice work," I said, leaning over to give him a hug while he was still on the piano bench.

We looked around. No doors had opened. No new passageways had appeared. Then we heard a small click.

Hyacinth turned to look at the closet. "I think the click came from there," she said.

We walked over, and Gabe pulled on one of the small door handles. The closet swung open.

Inside, there were dozens of long rectangular packages with labels on the ends for different songs. I recognized some words—*Figaro*, *Tosca*—but there was also "Happy Birthday to You," "The Magician's Trick," "Oranges and Apple Blossoms,"

"Captain's March," "For He's a Jolly Good Fellow" and "Danse Macabre"—a classical Halloween classic!

"Oh, some of these are opera songs!" said Gabe, reaching for one labeled "Nessun Dorma." "That's 'Let no one sleep' in Italian. One of the best arias of all time. It probably won't sound very good with just this dinky piano playing it, though."

I thought of the journal entry. "The piano isn't dinky, Gabe. Remember what Frances said: there's no such thing as a cheap trick."

Hyacinth ran her hands along the boxes. "Aunt Frances sounds so cool. I can see why Aunt Charlotte loved her."

"So what are these boxes, anyway? I'm not sure I get it," I said.

"I bet they're more cylinders!" said Hyacinth. "That play new songs! I bet we have to replace the roll that's in the piano now with one of these."

"Cool," Gabe and I said. Even after all these rooms, Charlotte could still delight us.

Hyacinth nodded. "Very cool," she said.

"So how do we figure out which one of these rolls we need?" said Gabe.

"It'll be the song she wrote for Frances, obviously!" I flapped my hands in excitement.

"But what is that? Maybe the clue is somewhere in there," Gabe said, pointing to the journal. Hyacinth handed it to him, and he looked at it for a long moment.

I looked back at the cabinet full of piano rolls. One title caught my eye. "'The Magician's Trick,'" I said. I grabbed it from the closet and handed it to Hyacinth. "You take a look."

She opened the box and took out the cylinder with the sheet music. The paper was tightly wound around the cylinder and had a seal holding it in place. The seal was stamped "C.F."

"Looks right," I said.

We took it to the piano and opened the lid. Gabe, with his careful fingers, took the seal off. We wound the paper through the machine, then closed the lid, stepped back and waited.

After a moment, the piano began to play, and Gabe whispered the chords and notes as they happened: "C, E, G, A, G, E. F, A, C, D, C, A. G-chord. D, B, G. F-chord." It was a short song, mostly ascending and descending notes, C-, G- and F-chords. It finished. We waited again.

"Nothing happened." I tried to stop from choking up. We were so close, but somehow we'd failed *again*?

"Let me try something," Gabe said. "Wind it up again."

Hyacinth set it up. The piano started to play, and Gabe played along with it, but in a lower register. When the piano hit a high C note, he played middle C. After a few more run-throughs, he and the pianola were perfectly in sync. Hyacinth and I started humming along.

"It's a duet," said Gabe. "The piano is playing one hand, and I'm playing the other."

Gabe and the piano reached the final note, and it hung in the air. We could still hear the piano roll turning. Gabe sat on the bench, watching it.

"What is it? Why didn't the piano roll stop when the music stopped?" I asked.

Gabe smiled. "Because the song ends on a rest."

Finally, the roll stopped turning and the pianola stood completely still.

There was a click and a whir from somewhere close by. I looked around, eager to see the hidden door. But then, nothing.

"I don't believe this!" I sighed.

Gabe's shoulders slumped, and he banged his elbows on the keys.

"Wait," said Hyacinth. "What if we did it right, but it just takes time? In that first room you were in"—she started flipping through her instruction book's pages—"the picture walls descend from the ceiling slowly, while you're supposed to be asleep. What if this room is supposed to be where we rest?"

"We don't have *time* to rest! We need to keep going, or how else will I get back for Halloween?"

Gabe straightened. "But, Zed, think about Charlotte and Frances—this room is all about them, right? Not just as professional collaborators, but as girlfriends or wives. This room is like"—he looked around at the flowers on the walls and the huge windows—"it's like a break from everything. Charlotte is telling us to rest. That's why the song ends on a *musical* rest."

"If we can't get out yet anyway, we might as well get some sleep," Hyacinth agreed.

I looked around. The cushions from the fainting couch did look comfy. Reluctantly, I nodded.

Hyacinth opened the closet with the sheet music rolls again and scrounged around. "Hey, look!" She pointed deep in the cupboard.

Hidden behind all the cylinders was a pile of pillows and blankets. We took them all out and arranged them on the floor. We let Gabe have the fainting-couch cushions because he was the hero of the hour. When I went back to close the closet, I saw a very yellowed and crumpled piece of paper resting on the ground where the bedding had been. I picked it up—it looked like it had been torn out of a journal much like the one we had been carrying around. I read it aloud: "*The lights are dimming, my dear. Take a rest. Our travels can wait. Let the sounds soothe you to sleep. I will see you in the morning. Love always, C.S.*"

"My heart," I said.

Hyacinth sniffled.

"Let's put on a lullaby," Gabe suggested.

I nodded. "You're the expert. You try."

He reached into the closet and pulled out a box labeled "Nocturne 6."

"This is a piano piece by Chopin!" he said giddily.

Hyacinth and I settled in while he put the music in the pianola. I gave Hyacinth my Frankenstein sweatshirt to sleep in. She wrinkled her nose but accepted it. Then she lay down.

"Oh, this is actually so warm, Zed."

"It's Frankenstein's creature's love," I said.

She laughed. "Maybe so. Goodnight, you guys."

The soft strains of a quiet piano melody floated in the air. Sort of like its own kind of ghost. I snuggled in and pictured Charlotte and Frances playing a duet on the piano, with Frances singing in her beautiful voice, the light of love shining on her face.

CHAPTER 18

GHOSTS AND SHIPS

Halloween morning. I swallowed my sadness. "Encore," I whispered to myself.

Gabe was already up, sitting on the fainting couch, munching on a muffin and leafing through the journal. Hyacinth was standing by the far wall, her trusty crowbar in her hand.

"Sleep okay, Gabe?" I asked.

"Not bad. You?"

"Ugh. I just had a horrible nightmare."

"Do tell."

"I was trying to catch a giant jack-o'-lantern. His carved head was filled with some Zed-level candy choices—all full-size bars. And some opera was playing in the background."

"Sounds like a beautiful dream."

"Ha. But every time I got closer, he would run away. I'd chase. He'd run. Over and over."

"What a jerk-o'-lantern!" Hyacinth called over her shoulder.

"I approve of that joke," I said. "Anyway, he ran through the doors of this house, then turned and gave a giant howl. The doors closed, and it started to rain candy corn." I shuddered at the memory.

"Aw," Gabe said. "Feeling a little sad about missing trick-or-treating?"

I wiped away a tear. "I just have to keep remembering we're here to help Sam and Jo. And Hyacinth too. I'm clinging to the hope that if we find some treasure, a bundle of cash, they'll also agree it should be a Dracula-themed ceremony."

"Um, what?" Gabe looked up from the journal. "I thought you were joking about that."

"Please, Gabe, I *never* joke about vampires."

"Oh, brother."

"Okay, you two." Hyacinth clapped her hands together. "Time to resume the search." She stepped aside, revealing a narrow opening in the wallpaper where the fountain motif had been.

"Where did that come from?" I asked.

"It was a sliding door. It just kind of appeared while we were sleeping," Gabe said. "Already opened. Well, opened a bit."

"I had to use the crowbar to pry it the rest of the way. There appears to be a small hallway leading to another door."

"Any ghosts munching on the floor?" I asked.

"No."

"Ah, well, I can still hope." I got up and grabbed a scone and an orange juice. Both were delicious. "The ghosts here sure can cook."

"I told you—Bertie does the cooking," said Hyacinth. "She dropped it through a secret slot in the wall this morning. That was one of the instructions Aunt C left behind. She was apparently a huge fan of a good breakfast."

"I love her even more," I said. "So shall we?" I slung my backpack over my shoulder, then put my hands on my hips, elbows out.

Gabe and Hyacinth linked their arms with mine, and we made our way down the new hallway.

"Lions and monsters and ghosts," I said.

"Oh my!" responded Hyacinth and Gabe.

"Let's hope the wizard is a wizard who will serve," I added. I looked down at my feet as I began my best Dorothy dance. "Hey, there's a pattern in the wood." The floor ahead of us was cut in the intricate pattern of a ship's deck. "I hope this isn't the floor plan for the *Titanic*," I said.

Hyacinth knelt and ran her fingers over the pattern. "This looks like some old-timey pirate ship, not the *Titanic*."

"Oooh, I bet it's the set plan for the deck of *The Flying Dutchman*," Gabe said.

"You mentioned that before. That's another opera, right?" I said.

"Yup. Wagner."

"A comedy?"

"Ha. No. It's all about a ghost ship that's cursed to sail the ocean forever."

"You had me at ghost ship! So what happens?"

"Every seven years, the captain goes ashore to search for a woman who will love him. He finally finds one, but then she dies."

"Laughs aplenty," I said. "So is this a puzzle we have to solve?"

Hyacinth stood up. "Not sure. It's all inlaid wood, but I can't find anything that moves or might be loose. And there's nothing in my instruction book about it."

The next door was only a few feet away on the other side of the ship. It was close enough that we could make out the shapes of ships, trains and even an early biplane carved into the frame.

"Trippy," I chuckled. "Get it? Because the door is all about ways to take a trip?"

"Yeah. I got it," Hyacinth said.

"But you didn't laugh?"

"No. I didn't. Are they always like this, Gabe?"

"Sometimes they're funnier," Gabe said with a shrug.

"Thanks for the support, pal." I frowned.

"I guess we need to do something with those shapes to make the door open?" Gabe suggested.

"Only one way to find out. Let's go!"

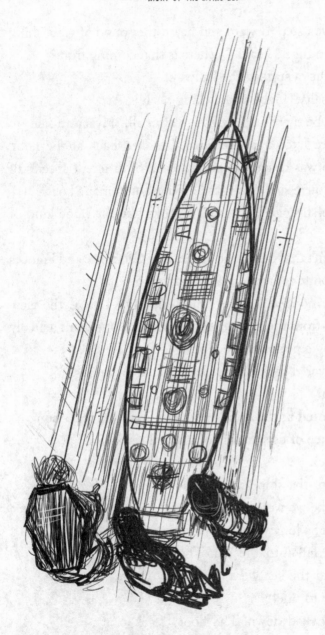

I took a step forward and heard the sound of whooshing water. "Strange," I said. "Where is that coming from?"

A light mist filled the hallway.

"It's salty," Gabe said, licking his lips.

"Maybe there's a puzzle here after all," Hyacinth said.

Before I took another step, I looked back at the floor. The ship was beautiful and made up of different species of wood. "You're sure this is the Flying Dutchman's boat?"

Gabe shrugged. "I mean, it looks like the same kind of ship."

"Wasn't that one of the operas that Charlotte and Frances worked on together?" Hyacinth asked.

Gabe nodded. "Funny thing, though. This is the view you'd get from up above the stage, not the one you'd actually see during a performance."

"Above?" I looked up. "Gabe, you are a genius."

"I am?"

I pointed at the ceiling—a perfect mirror reflection of the three of us standing on the hallway floor stared back.

Except the ship was gone. It looked like we were standing on one end of a long wooden board, about to fall into the sea. The board and the sea were moving from side to side.

We looked down. The floor

was the same outline of a ship. We looked up. It was like we were standing above rolling waves.

"That is seriously weird," I said.

"So what are we supposed to do?" Gabe asked.

I took another step, then looked up. On the floor, my foot was somewhere on the bow of the ship. But up above, I'd put one foot into the ocean. The floor below us tilted suddenly, sending us reeling. We steadied ourselves against the wall, and the floor pitched and rolled like it was trying to shake us off.

"Okay, rule number one: don't step in the ocean."

"Thanks, Captain Obvious!" Hyacinth said. "Lucky for me, I know how to skateboard."

She was doing a good job of keeping herself steady and upright. But I was starting to feel seasick.

"My dad took us canoeing once," Gabe said. "And I stood up in the canoe, and this is what happened. I capsized it and lost my fave pair of sneakers."

"So how do we un-capsize this boat?" I yelled.

The floor pitched so hard it revealed a gap, and you could see *beneath* the floor. I craned my neck. A green mist floated over a giant pool of murky water far below us. The face of an old sea captain appeared in the pool. He smiled and beckoned for us to join him. When we met the creepy ghost in the sun room, I'd wanted to talk to it. But there wasn't a single atom of me that wanted to talk to *this* ghost, who clearly had only one thought in mind: trapping three kids forever in a watery grave.

"No, thanks!" I said, and jerked myself upright. I looked at the ceiling again. "Rule number two: walk without looking down."

While looking up, I moved my feet to follow the board in the ceiling. Gabe and Hyacinth did the same, and the floor settled again. Then, above us, the board shifted to the left, and we had to jump quickly so the floor we were standing on stayed steady. The board stayed in place, and we each moved one step forward. Then the board moved two steps to the right. Hyacinth and I stepped right, but Gabe got his feet tangled and fell. The floor beneath us pitched again. I grabbed him just as he was about to slide down into the deep, and I dragged him back next to us, hugging him tight. I looked up—we were all standing on the board again. Safe for now.

"Thanks, Zed," he said.

"Rule number three: we need to look at things differently. Again."

"Up is down and down is up," Hyacinth said.

"Everyone keep walking, but step *only* where the board on the ceiling is. That's how we cross. It's showing us the only safe path to the door."

What followed was one of the weirdest things I've ever experienced. It's hard to describe it. It might seem like an easy job, walking while looking up, but it is not. My neck was killing me. We almost got thrown into the sea at least three more times before we finally made it to the other side.

Once there, the waves stopped waving. The mist stopped misting. The door clicked and opened. Hyacinth the skater-ghost-girl had gotten there first, and she coughed and waved her hand in front of her face.

"The air smells kind of stale," she said.

"Musty," Gabe agreed.

"I'm not sure anyone's made it this far before," she said.

Gabe and I looked at each other and smiled.

"Maybe missing Halloween isn't so bad—if you're with your best fiend," I said.

"I think you mean 'friend,'" Hyacinth corrected.

"No, they don't," Gabe said.

We took a deep breath and pushed the door open all the way.

CHAPTER 19

THE QUEEN OF THE NIGHT SKY

Gabe and I both love maps—making them and following them—but nothing could have prepared us for the room we now stepped into. A giant map of the world covered everything in the room. And I mean *everything*.

The walls, the domed ceiling and even the floor were covered in ornately painted countries, oceans, mountains, lakes and rivers. There were five doors built into the opposite wall, which was covered with most of Europe and the Atlantic Ocean.

"Really? No doors in any other rooms, and now this one has *five*?" I said.

"An embarrassment of riches," said Gabe.

I turned to Hyacinth. "Any ideas?"

She held out her crowbar. "Just the usual one."

"Absolutely not," said Gabe. "Who knows what we could

damage if we tried that. This place is too beautiful to act like a can opener on all these doors."

"Suit yourself." Hyacinth shrugged.

There was only one piece of furniture facing us: a wicker wheelchair I didn't see at first because it was painted blue like the ocean, which took up most of the floor in front of us. Next to the chair sat an antique globe in a wooden stand.

"This is fantastic!" I said in an awed whisper.

"So what are we looking for to get out of here?" Gabe wondered. "The chair's gotta be part of the solution, right?"

"Probably. Did you read anything useful in the journal before we came in here?" asked Hyacinth.

"More love letters. But these maps ... might be telling us to look for places Charlotte and Frances visited," Gabe said.

"Okay, but which places?" Hyacinth asked. "I mean, this map shows pretty much every city on the globe." I took my backpack off my shoulders and put it on the floor. I unzipped its pocket, pulled out the journal and handed it to Gabe.

Gabe opened the journal. "Charlotte says they traveled together a lot for work. Once her career took off, she and

Frances designed sets for companies all over the place." He cleared his throat and read us one of the letters:

1906—

Spent all day in the company of Xavier and his wife, and consequently felt irritable and tired, and decided to walk home—only to run into the mailman carrying the most precious parcel. Your postcard and small treasures had the effect of a healing tonic on my dark mood.

There was another letter with some interesting news: Paris is bringing Das Rheingold back to French audiences next year. Of course, for such a grand production they require equally grand sets. Well, who better to help me design those than my own magician?

The next stage in our journey, perhaps?

This next part is a secret, so read it in a private place, away from prying eyes.

I will make myself clearer and reveal the secret I've been keeping from you for some months now: I've purchased some land and have been making a home, with both of us in mind. I do not wish to be parted from you, ever again. Physical distance is nothing; I mean spiritually. Will you stay with me in this house, for all intents and purposes, as my wife? You needn't say anything now, but do think on it. I'm also concealing in this letter a kiss, only for you.

"The next stage on their journey," I said. "This was a really busy few years, following that letter."

Gabe flipped to a spread with many sketches of buildings. "These are all different opera houses they worked at. Here's La Scala—that's the opera house in Milan. Also the Palais Garnier, or the Paris opera house. A classic."

Hyacinth and I exchanged a glance. "Yeah, he's a bit weird," I said.

She snorted. "You both are. Do you notice something about the cities he's talking about?"

I looked around at the giant map. "Oh, wow! Milan, Paris—those both have stars painted on them."

Hyacinth nodded.

"Go on, Gabe," I encouraged.

He listed more cities. Then he said, "I don't recognize this one, but the journal says it's Madrid?"

I pointed to a spot near my shoulder. "There's a star on Madrid!" I ran my finger over it. The surface of the star stuck out a bit from the wall. "I think it might actually be a button!"

"So maybe we push them in some sequence, like the keys on that piano?" Hyacinth said.

Gabe continued his opera-house tour of the world. "This next sketch looks like the Bolshoi Theatre in Moscow. That's where Shostakovich's *The Nose* premiered!"

I looked wayyy up on the ceiling to find the star on Moscow. "That's much too high for me, even if I stood on that chair."

"Maybe if we were adult-size?" said Hyacinth.

She walked over to the wheelchair and tried to move it, but it stayed put. She sat down and tried to turn the wheels. She rocked slightly from side to side, but the chair didn't shift.

"Hmmm," she said finally. "It's bolted to the floor."

She got up and began walking around the chair while I looked for more stars. I spotted a few—one in New York (behind us on the other wall) and a second in Prague (just above the fourth door from the left).

Then I heard a squeak.

"Was that a mouse?"

"No," Hyacinth said. "This chair and this globe are bolted to the floor. The globe doesn't spin, and the chair's wheels don't move either. But look at this." She gripped the side of the wheelchair and pulled it toward her. A circular section of the floor beneath it slowly rotated, squeaking and groaning.

"That's cool. Why does it do that?" said Gabe.

She rotated it a little bit more, then smiled. She pointed to the globe and then at the wall. "I turned it so that the locations on the globe match up with where they're painted on the walls."

"She's right," Gabe said. "England lines up with England, Spain with Spain, and so on."

"And when the locations are lined up like this, you'll notice where the chair is facing."

"Second door from the left," I said.

"That was a pretty cool puzzle," Hyacinth said as she walked to the door.

But something didn't feel right. It was too easy. We'd just almost died falling into a haunted ocean. Could this really be so simple? I looked at the chair, the globe and the stars.

Then I saw it. Sticking out from under the stand for the globe was an electrical cord. Since when does a globe need power? And hadn't Bertie said that electricity was a very expensive novelty? So why spend that much money just to wire a globe? Something wasn't adding up.

As Hyacinth began to turn the handle on the second door, I shouted, "WAIT!!!!"

She froze with the door just about to open. One more half turn would have ended any chance to find the treasure or discover the rest of Charlotte and Frances's love story. I'm not even sure which I cared about more now.

Hyacinth let go of the doorknob and released a long, slow breath. "So this isn't the right door?"

"It might be. But it's also possible this was another clever misdirection." I nodded toward the globe. "That's not an ordinary globe."

"Meaning?" Gabe asked.

I pointed at the base. "Why does an antique globe have a cord?" I paused. "The answer, my friends, is because it's a lamp."

"So how do we turn it on?" Hyacinth asked, walking over.

We looked all around the chair and the globe but couldn't find a switch.

"There're no switches on the walls either," Gabe said.

"Or are there?" I said with a smile. "There are no light *switches* in any of the rooms."

"Huh?" said Gabe.

Hyacinth smiled too. "That's right. These old houses all have buttons."

I nodded. "And we already know there are buttons on the walls."

Gabe looked around in amazement. Now it was time to show off what else I'd learned and put it all together.

I cleared my throat. "So we know that the last opera Charlotte worked on—her triumph—was *The Magic Floop*."

"Flute," Gabe said.

Okay, my attention-paying was lacking some focus.

"Whatever. And then she went into seclusion after designing the set for the Queen of the Night. The one you love so much."

He nodded. "It's amazing."

"Where was that opera staged?"

Gabe didn't need to pull out his notebook. "Vienna."

"And I remember from the picture room that the first opera they worked on together was *Toffee*."

"You've got Halloween on the brain. It was *Tosca*."

"And where was that?"

"In Milan, at La Scala."

I nodded. "Okay, I have an idea. Hyacinth, get ready to press the star on Vienna—their last opera. And, Gabe, on Milan—their first."

They both walked over and hovered their fingers above each button.

"This room is about the beginning and the end of their journey together."

I took a deep breath and signaled for Gabe to press Milan. He did, and as I'd suspected, all the lights turned off, throwing us into complete darkness.

No, not complete darkness. A silvery mist appeared, hovering in the wheelchair, as if a silent figure had joined us, sitting, waiting, watching.

"Is-s-s . . . that a gh-gh . . . ?" Gabe was too scared to speak.

"Frances?" I said. I took a step forward, hoping to speak to her, to ask for her help.

There was a click as Hyacinth pushed the button for Vienna before my signal. The globe lit up, sending pinpricks of light throughout the room. The ghost shimmered, and I reached out to touch her hand, but she was gone.

I turned to Hyacinth and Gabe and pointed to the wheelchair. "I think I know why Charlotte stopped working and went into seclusion. Frances got sick. Charlotte quit everything to care for her. Her bright star. Her own Queen of the Night."

Hyacinth gasped and covered her mouth with her hands. "That is so sad," she finally said, blinking hard and staring at the empty chair.

Gabe sniffled. I did too. The room suddenly felt cold as we stood silently under a star-filled night sky.

Gabe was the first to speak. "It's beautiful." It was.

"I can see why that Queen of the Night set was so famous," I said.

Gabe shook his head. "This is nothing compared to what that was like. This is good, but I've seen illustrations based on the real thing, and it was . . . wow."

"Better than this?" said Hyacinth in disbelief.

"Yeah," said Gabe. "People who saw the opera described it as like sitting under a shimmering dome of golden light."

Gabe was right—this was nice . . . but shimmering? Not quite.

I was reminded of the beginning of our own journey, when the frame around Charlotte's portrait had suddenly radiated like gold. Bertie had said that was due to the reflective paint being hit with spotlighting. Yet another magic trick. Suddenly, I knew how to solve the room. Spotlights!

"We have to move the globe and the chair a little more." I began rotating the platform bit by bit. There was a sudden flash, like lightning, as the pinprick lights from the globe lined up with the stars over the cities on the map.

It was magic.

The room was now bathed in a glowing golden light, as if we'd walked into the middle of the most radiant sky ever.

"*This* is what I was talking about," said Gabe.

Now the chair was in the correct position. It was facing the third door.

"Nice deducing, Zed," said Hyacinth.

"*That* was a team effort from start to finish," I said. "So let's see where the door leads us."

We walked together to the doorstep, soaked in the golden light.

"A little slice of heaven," said Hyacinth.

I looked back and was sure I could make out the ghostly shadow of Frances in the wheelchair, wrapped in a shawl, looking thin and frail.

"Oh no!" I said. "Frances didn't just get sick—she . . . she died."

The door clicked open.

And the floor beneath us gave way, sending us spiraling down into darkness.

CHAPTER 20

CHERUBO THE GIANT AND THE DISAPPEARING HORSE

We slid down a metal chute. The trapdoor we'd fallen through banged shut above us.

"I can't believe we were wrong!" I howled as I spun around and down.

Gabe was just plain howling. "Noooooooooooooo!!!!"

Hyacinth must have been somewhere with us, but I couldn't see her or hear her.

I was getting dizzy and had started to feel sick when all of a sudden, I was tossed into the air.

I flailed my arms and then landed on a pile of straw. I could feel bits of it poking through my sweater. I knew at least one other kid was about to be thrown into the same spot, so I scrambled forward.

"AAAAAAH!!!!" Gabe yelled as he flew through the air, then landed behind me.

He tumbled forward and plowed into my back. That

pushed us both off the edge, and we landed on a hard floor with a thud.

"Ouch!" we said together.

"I can't see a thing," Gabe complained. "And my butt hurts."

"Another advantage of thick sweaters is that they absorb some of the force of an unexpected impact. Lights would be helpful, though!" I yelled to the ghosts.

There was a popping sound and the smell of gas.

"That doesn't smell good," I said.

A series of torches sprung to life along a nearby stone wall. We could see some of the room now. It was filled with boxes and other strange objects I couldn't make out in the shadows.

More lights began burning, and the dancing flames made the stone walls seem as if they were also swaying and moving.

"Not again." Gabe tucked his knees close to his chest. "I don't like this place anymore."

"You didn't like it from the beginning. Maybe we *did* pick the right door?" I realized Hyacinth was still nowhere to be seen. "Or maybe we were duped by a ghost? A ghost named Hyacinth!"

"I AM NOT A GHOST!" Hyacinth's face peeped over the edge of the stacked hay bales.

"Maybe you're a traitor!" I said, pointing a finger accusingly. "You wanted to keep the treasure for your family, so you tricked us into falling through a trapdoor!"

"Then why would I be here too?"

I stopped wagging my finger. "You are a very clever ghost."

Our argument was interrupted by a cackle from somewhere off to our left.

"Who's there?" Hyacinth called.

The cackling grew louder.

More lights now flickered on, and we could finally see the whole room. It was enormous and windowless, and we could see the source of the laughter: a giant doll's head sticking out of the top of what appeared to be a large wooden barrel. The hinged mouth ground up and down, the laughter rising and falling with the creepy jaws.

It turned to face us and blinked.

Gabe screamed.

The doll screamed back and then glided toward us.

"We're all gonna die!" Gabe yelled. He grabbed Hyacinth's hand to pull himself back up onto the hay, but instead he pulled her down to the floor with us.

The baby head continued to come closer . . . and closer.

"RUN!" Hyacinth screamed.

We ran, hugging the stone walls like shadows. The laughter pitched higher as the doll head sped up.

I tripped over something and stumbled to the floor. Gabe and Hyacinth fell on top of me. The head was now almost upon us! It gave a deep grinding screech, a metallic *SCREAM*— and then stopped. The laughter ended mid-cackle.

I looked up. The head loomed over us, with the flame of the nearby lamps casting one side in deep shadow. It looked demented. Its now unmoving eyes locked onto us, three kids lying like ghost kibble on the ground. It was waiting for any sign of movement before it jumped!

"That's not helping," Gabe said.

"What?"

"You saying all that stuff out loud, about kibble and it waiting to jump."

"I was saying all that out loud?"

"Yeah."

"Well, it was pretty good material, though. If we ever get out of here, we'll be able to up our radio-interview game. But this thing hasn't moved at all, so maybe it has—haha—given up the ghost."

Gabe groaned.

I resumed my narration. "Zed bravely stood up and tapped the head. It sounded hollow."

"Zed's head would sound hollow," said Hyacinth.

"Shh," I said. "Stop ruining the moment."

"Booooo-m," said Gabe. "That was you blowing up the spooky vibe."

A bit of paint flaked off the head and fell to the floor. "I'm not sure why this doll stopped," I said. "But it seems pretty harmless now."

Hyacinth stuck out her tongue at the head. "Who's laughing now?"

I almost expected it to quickly attack her. It didn't.

Gabe used his sleeve to wipe some dust and grime off a metal sign on the barrel under the head.

"It says 'Cherubo, the Wonder Giant, carved from a single piece of an ancient sequoia. Knows your past. Tells your future.'"

"Maybe it was about to tell us what happens next! And we killed it!" I moaned. "Wait, did you say Cherubo?"

"Yeah, why?"

"I remember that name from somewhere," I said, racking my brains.

"I think Cherubo sprung a fatal leak," Gabe said. "Look, there's a trail of oil on the floor behind it."

"Hmmm. Sure it's not ectoplasm?"

"Smells like your brother Jimi's cologne."

"Definitely oil, then." I went back to thinking about where I'd heard the name Cherubo before. "Wait! I remember now. Frances the Fantastic! The poster from the maquette room!"

"Frances the Fantastic? That's also over here, on a poster on this wall," said Hyacinth, pointing to a spot in the gloom. "See?"

We walked to where she was pointing.

"Oh! You can read this whole poster here," I said.

Frances the Fantastic, the Greatest Magician in the World . . . RETURNS for one final show!
Featuring feats of unimaginable danger.
You will gasp!
You will be amazed!
Cherubo the Giant!
The Disappearing Horse!
BEWARE!
The Guillotine of Trust.
BEWARE!
The Seven Flaming Swords! A whirling circle of fire and steel!

"The Guillotine of Trust and the Disappearing Horse? Sounds weird and corny, not scary," said Hyacinth.

I cocked my head. "Hmm. There's a note on the poster. It looks like Charlotte's handwriting." I narrowed my eyes. "It says 'Losing you felt like losing a limb. Once the sickness came, no magic could save you.'"

The flames flickered.

"There's something here too," said Gabe. With shaking fingers, he pulled out a piece of paper tucked in behind the poster. "It's a newspaper clipping. It says that Frances disappeared at the end of this show and was never seen again." The newspaper fluttered in his hand, as if stirred by an imperceptible breeze.

"Now we know why she disappeared," said Hyacinth, choking up. "She was too sick to continue."

I nodded. "But let's focus on the puzzle," I said. "We have a poster with Charlotte's handwriting and a newspaper clipping. This is clearly the clue."

"I agree," said Gabe. "But what do we do with them?"

We turned away from the poster and took in the room around us. It was mostly just trunks and boxes.

"Well, we know Cherubo is from the magic show," said Hyacinth. "It was mentioned on the poster. So presumably these boxes have more magic props in them."

I spotted something out of the corner of my eye. It was a guillotine on a high platform, looming above the rest of the boxes.

"The guillotine from the poster," I said.

"And look up there," said Hyacinth, pointing even higher than the guillotine.

Gabe and I squinted and saw a door far, far above our heads.

"That door looks totally unreachable," I said, "even if we climb up on the guillotine platform. It's like we're trapped in a clown's dungeon."

"SHHH! Don't insult the ghosts!" said Gabe—but it was too late.

There was a hiss and then a whir from the far end of the room. We looked over. One of the giant boxes had opened: a huge wheel rose up, then burst into flames.

"The whirling circle of fire and steel!" Hyacinth yelled.

"I see the fire. But what's the steel?" I asked.

A second later, a large flaming sword flew out of the spinning circle, straight toward my head.

CHAPTER 21

THE GUILLOTINE OF TRUST

I'd like to say that I ducked like some sweater-wearing super-hero, but I'm not that fast.

Luckily, the sword *just* missed the top of my head and jammed into the mortar between two stones, vibrating as it swung back and forth. *That's* when I ducked. So did Hyacinth and Gabe. The stone put out the fire on the blade.

"If I were an inch taller, that would have been curtains!" I exclaimed.

Hyacinth was clearly rattled. "This place isn't supposed to be *this* dangerous!!"

"Maybe the further you get, the more the ghosts try to stop you?" said Gabe.

"No, I think this was one of Frances's magic tricks. Where she dodged the Seven Flaming Swords, like the poster says," I said.

"And the house wants us to do *that*? No, thanks," Gabe said.

Suddenly, another sword flew through the air, piercing a box a few feet away. We were, for the moment, safely hidden between a huge stack of boxes.

"I *don't* believe in ghosts, I *don't* believe in ghosts," said Gabe, eyes closed.

I was confused. So far, the journal and the rooms had all been showing us ways to escape, helping us reveal the story of Charlotte and Frances. Just to kill us in the dingy old basement? It didn't make sense.

A third sword hit a spot on the wall and bounced off with a clang, falling to the ground.

"Hyacinth, we know this place has been breaking down, right?"

"Yes. Doors haven't opened the way they should. Strange sounds, like grinding gears, come from the floors and walls. Killer doll heads spring leaks. Stuff like that."

"So what if all this down here was just supposed to scare us? But because it's been sitting in this musty basement for a hundred years, it's going haywire."

Gabe opened his eyes and joined the discussion. "Like some of the old radios my dad picks up at yard sales. He'll turn them on, and sometimes the tubes blow up. Or the wires have been chewed on by mice and sometimes they spark."

"So you mean this is *really* dangerous?" Hyacinth asked.

"Or it could also be angry ghosts," I said. "Toying with us?"

I was about to elaborate on this point when another two swords came flying, lodging themselves in the eye sockets of Cherubo's head. The flames began to lick at its eyes, which quickly set the head on fire.

"If we die here, does that mean we get to haunt this cool place too?" I wondered out loud.

"How about we *don't* die here?!" Hyacinth shouted.

"Okay, suit yourself. So what's the plan?"

"We have to get to that door!"

"I got that," I said. "It's the 'how' part I'm having trouble visualizing."

"We could stack some boxes underneath, maybe?" she suggested.

"Worth a try," said Gabe. He started scrambling away on all fours. Then he turned back to look at us. "Hey, I think there's a pathway through here, between these boxes."

We followed, crawling between the boxes like rats in a maze. A sword shot from the wheel straight up to the ceiling and right back down to the floor. This thing was really busted up. We heard the wheel slow down.

"Is that it? I counted seven," said Gabe over his shoulder.

I opened my mouth to say I'd counted six, but before I could get that out, the seventh and final sword streaked through the air above us like a shooting star . . . and landed squarely in the hay bale, which immediately began to burn.

We stood up and looked at the hay, wondering what we should do about it.

"You know, they say smoke can be more dangerous than fire," Gabe offered helpfully.

"There's got to be water somewhere," Hyacinth said. "With all those pipes we've had to maintain."

But a quick scan of the ceiling didn't reveal anything promising. So it was either escape or join Frances and Charlotte in the great beyond.

We moved faster standing up and quickly reached the boxes under the door.

"That's gonna take a lot of boxes to reach up there," I said.

"Well, it all starts with one," Gabe replied.

"Another one of your dad's sayings?"

"You know it."

We tried to push and lift the boxes to make a kind of staircase, but it turned out they were way too heavy to move.

I fell to the floor, wiping sweat off my brow.

"Aunt Charlotte didn't make anything easy, did she?" said Hyacinth.

"So how do we get up there?" I asked.

The smoky air started to burn my throat. The fires weren't that big yet, but with no windows, the room was starting to fill up with smoke.

I thought back to the poster of Frances's last magic show. "Nothing in this house has been put there by chance," I said. "Everything is a clue. What are we missing here?"

"We already met Cherubo," Gabe said with a shudder.

"Check," I agreed.

"And the Seven Flaming Swords," Hyacinth added.

"But the poster also mentioned the Disappearing Horse and the Guillotine of Trust."

"The horse appears to have disappeared already—I don't see it anywhere," Hyacinth said.

Honestly, her ability to crack a well-timed *bon mot* was growing on me.

"So that leaves . . . the guillotine."

We'd seen that earlier, and it was now only a few feet away, on a raised platform. The blade glistened high up in between the wooden posts.

"That still looks sharp," I said. "What are we supposed to do with it?"

We clambered over and up some wooden steps, then walked around the contraption, searching for clues. Gabe got on his hands and knees and looked underneath, while Hyacinth checked the platform itself for trapdoors.

I was looking at the place where the blade would fall. The choppy "goodbye head" bit.

"That's odd," I said, moving my head from side to side and up and down.

Gabe popped up. "What's odd?"

"If you look from the front of the guillotine—the bit where you put your head—you can see that it's lower than the bench you lie on behind it. But you should be at the same level, right?"

"Why do you keep saying 'you'?"

"Fine, the place where 'one' might put 'one's' head. From down below, they appear to be at the same level, but when you get up here, you can see they're not."

I crouched down and peered through the hole in the stocks. Something inside was glowing faintly.

"Hey, it's a key! A ghostly key!"

I instantly realized the problem: to get the key, you had to put your hand through the hole. The hole where the blade would drop. Like I said, the choppy bit.

"The Guillotine of Trust," I said morosely. "Nice one, Charlotte. I get it."

"'Losing you felt like losing a limb,'" Gabe quoted. "Someone has to be brave enough to put their hand inside and grab that key."

"Give it a try, Zed." Hyacinth motioned with both hands, like she was shooing me forward to my doom.

"Why me?!"

"Because you're standing right next to the hole!"

I gulped. She did have a point. But we'd just been attacked by a malfunctioning doll's head and a whirring sword-throwing wheel. Who knew if this thing worked?

Time was running out. The smoke was building every second we hesitated.

"Who knows how many generations of mice have been gnawing on the rope?" I said, pointing to the cord that suspended the blade. "Plus, I really like this hand."

"You haven't even put a hand inside yet!" Hyacinth said.

"I like BOTH hands!!"

"It's another magic trick," Gabe said. "It's about the appearance of danger, not real danger."

"Tell that to the sword that almost gave me a haircut," I coughed. And I didn't even want to say my big lingering question out loud: Once I got the key, how did we get up to that door?

I closed my eyes, took a deep breath and stuck my hand through the hole.

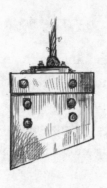

CHAPTER 22

OUT OF THE FRYING PAN ... INTO THE FLOOD

The rope holding the blade gave a twang like a plucked banjo string.

I jerked my hand back out quickly.

"Did you get the key?" asked Gabe.

"Um, no."

"Get out of the way," Hyacinth said. "I'm already a ghost, so the blade can't chop off my arm anyway."

"I knew it!" I said.

"I'm kidding, Zed!"

She thrust her hand inside and reached for the key.

"There's nothing in here!" she said.

She reached deeper and began rummaging around inside. The blade vibrated slightly as the rope played more horrible banjo music.

"I can't feel any key," Hyacinth said. "It's another illusion!" She continued to search inside.

"Um, guys?" Gabe pointed up toward the door above us.

We turned. The door had opened, and a bright light was shining through. And below the door, a wooden horse on a pole was rising out of one of the boxes.

"The *Appearing* Horse!" Hyacinth yelled. She pulled her hand out of the hole. The door closed, and the horse began to drop back into the box.

"You're kidding me," she said. "So someone has to stay behind with their hand in this thing?"

"I guess that's like what happened in real life," I said. "Frances left, and Charlotte stayed behind in a dark place with only memories of their life together."

"Searching for some magic to bring her back," Gabe said.

"So who stays here, and who goes up there?" I asked.

Hyacinth gave a long sigh. "My family got us into this mess. *I* should stay behind so you two can get out."

"Can't we just jam something into the hole so we can *all* escape?" Gabe suggested.

"That's a great idea!" I said.

But a quick scan of the room didn't reveal anything small enough to fit. The swords, which might have worked, were now behind a growing wall of flame and smoke.

"Wait!" Hyacinth said. "My crowbar!"

She put it in the hole, and we all turned to look at the horse. Nothing happened.

"We keep having good ideas, and they keep doing absolutely nothing for us," I said. I tried to yell that, but my lungs were filling with smoke.

Hyacinth shook her head. "Look, we're out of time. Charlotte said someone in her family would have to help find the treasure. This is me helping."

"This is ridiculous," I said.

But Gabe put a hand on my shoulder. "The quicker we get up there"—he pointed at the door—"the quicker we can look for something to get Hyacinth out."

"Exactly," Hyacinth said. "Like a rope or a ladder!"

I nodded, but I wasn't happy.

She did her best to smile at me. "Maybe we'll meet again. I might even be a real ghost next time."

Gabe and I hugged her.

"No, we're going to get you out of this," I promised. "Although you would make a great ghost."

"I agree. Now go!"

We ran to the box under the door. Hyacinth waved and then put her arm back through the hole. The lid opened, and the horse began to rise.

"After you," I said.

Gabe climbed up onto the saddle and then helped me climb up behind him.

"This is definitely the weirdest merry-go-round I've ever been on," I said as the horse began to rise.

"I can just see this trick being used in *Don Giovanni* or for the entrance of the Queen of the Night," Gabe said.

Looking down, we could see Hyacinth coughing into her sleeve and the fire starting to spread to more boxes.

The smoke curled into different shapes and forms. I swear I saw the ghostly outline of a woman making her way toward the guillotine.

"Faster!" I said, kicking my heels into the side of the stuffed horse.

We continued to rise. The smoke was billowing around

us, flowing up through the door and into whatever awaited us in the next room.

Finally, the horse reached the open door, but we could barely see anything beyond. It was too bright.

"Maybe we did die?" I joked.

"Pretty sure people aren't taken up to heaven on a stuffed horse," Gabe replied.

"Although that would be amazing!"

The horse stopped. There was still a gap of a few feet between us and what, in the bright light, looked like a small landing made of polished marble.

"Another leap of faith?" Gabe asked.

"So it would appear."

Gabe stood up on the horse's back and swung his arms back and forth a few times. Then he jumped and landed on the marble. He stumbled but then stood up straight. I could barely make out his shape in the bright light.

"Jump, Zed!"

I stood on the horse's back and got ready to jump. But just as I was about to push off, I heard a loud twang from below. Hyacinth screamed.

Immediately, the horse began to drop.

And water began to fall from the ceiling.

"JUMP!" Gabe shouted.

I jumped, but I was too far down to reach to the doorway with my feet. Instead, I threw my arms forward, hoping Gabe would catch me.

He did, gripping my arms as I slammed chest first into the stone wall.

"OOF!" All the air got knocked out of my lungs.

Gabe planted a foot against the doorframe and held on to me tight.

"Zed! Scramble up!"

I could barely breathe, but I did my best to flail my feet against the wall. Luckily, the stones were all rough and uneven, so it was easy to get a foothold. But the falling water was making it all slippery.

"PULL!" I wheezed.

Gabe leaned back, pulling me along with him. My hand began to slip out of his, then it did . . .

I reached frantically for anything to hold on to, and my fingers caught the edge of a large pocket on his pants! I gripped it and stopped falling. It seemed to take forever, but bit by bit, Gabe was able to shimmy backward, pulling me through the doorway, still holding on to his pocket.

"I'll never joke about your pockets again," I said as I lay flat on the floor, breathing deeply. "Those are real sturdy pants."

"What happened to Hyacinth?"

"I don't know. I heard a twang and a scream."

We ran to the doorway and peered down.

"Can you see her through the rain?" I asked Gabe.

"Monsoon is more like it," he said. "There's water falling everywhere. I can't see anything."

"Like a million tears," I said.

"I think it's putting the fires out, at least. But also the torches!"

"HYACINTH!!!!" we both yelled.

But there was no answer.

The door slammed shut.

CHAPTER 23

THE UN-GREEN GREENHOUSE

We pushed and pushed, but the door refused to open.

"She's trapped in there!"

"Bertie said there'd always be a button somewhere we could push to call for help, right?"

We began frantically looking around for any sign of one, but we couldn't find anything. It was hard to tell where to look. The room we were in was the largest and the strangest yet.

Walls of glass rose up, towering above us and meeting in a giant arched glass ceiling, which seemed impossibly far away.

"It's a greenhouse," said Gabe the plant lover. Then he shook himself out of his reverie. "If there's no button, we gotta find a rope or something. Maybe there's a hose or ladder here."

We split up and began to search everywhere. There were tons of dead plants and cracked pots, bright and low-hanging lamps, but nothing that would help us pull Hyacinth up from the basement. We tried again to open the door, but it didn't budge. We screamed and yelled her name and put our ears to the door, but we couldn't hear anything. The wood was too thick.

Exhausted, I leaned my forehead against the door in defeat. "We quit!" I yelled to no one. "Come get us! We want to leave, okay? We want to go back to the basement. Please! Please let us back." I started to cry and banged my forehead against the door in frustration.

Gabe looked around again. "There must be something in here that we missed. We need to stop freaking out and figure this out. Hyacinth is relying on us to be smart."

I wiped my nose on my sleeve and straightened up. "You're right. Panicking won't help us."

He was rocking on his feet, thinking. "Let's start with what we know. Hyacinth is trapped in the basement. It's raining down there, which will put out the fires. She's on a raised platform if the water starts to flood. She needs to get up to the door we came through."

I nodded. "If we can't find a ladder or a rope or a way to get this door open, maybe we need to solve this room like we did the others."

We began to walk deeper into the greenhouse, going more slowly and checking everything for clues or another way to get her out.

I looked up at the ceiling again. There was no sky, no sun. It was completely blocked by wooden slats.

"Hey, Gabe, remember that peaked roof we saw the first night? I think that's where we are. Underneath that peak, somewhere in the middle of the manor."

"But if this is a greenhouse, why hide the sun?" he asked, pointing at the wooden cover.

"It looks like there used to be *some* sun." I gestured at the rows and rows of pots, planters and raised garden beds.

Gabe looked like he wanted to cry. "These plants are all dead." He walked up to an enormous porcelain pot and read the small sign. "There used to be a Trinidadian banana plant here. Now it's just a grizzled stump."

There were more remains of ferns, trees, tropical plants.

"They're all dead. No sun. No water."

"For a hundred years," I added.

There was still no sign of the promised button.

"What do you think Charlotte wants us to see?"

We walked around the marble floors, looking at everything.

"Hey, this is *real* marble," I said, feeling the difference between it and the fake tile I'd cracked at the foot of the grand staircase. This floor was harder, and my feet made a different sound walking on it.

Gabe rapped on a white metal girder. It vibrated, giving a satisfying metallic hum. "And these are real solid steel. This whole place is still in amazing shape . . . except for the plants."

The floor was divided by the planters and pots, almost like mini rooms. The marble path kept starting and stopping at odd angles. There was no straight route. We followed the marble tiles between the dead plants, but we could see only a few feet ahead of us, no matter which way we faced. I couldn't shake the feeling we were being watched. But the greenhouse was as silent as a tomb, the only sound our feet on the floor.

After a sharp turn, we were suddenly in a circular clearing with a low curved wall in the middle.

Gabe walked up to it slowly. "In case it's a trap," he said.

"Or it might also be haunted."

We walked around the outside of the wall, running our hands over the smooth cool tiles.

"It's not a circle," I said. "There's an indentation here. This is shaped like a heart!"

Gabe grabbed the top and pulled himself up, peering

over the edge. "It's beautiful inside too. The whole inside is filled with a tile mosaic of plants and birds."

"But what is it?"

"A fountain, I think. There's some staining, like a water ring, around the top of the basin."

"So it used to work?"

I leaned against the fountain and took it all in. The story Charlotte had wanted us to discover.

"This is it. This is the final room," I said.

Gabe lowered himself down from the edge of the fountain. "Why do you think that?"

"Every room we've been in—even the front stairs—was made to look fantastic, but each one was falling apart. Rotting wood on the porch and floors. Fake marble. Fake stone pillars."

Gabe nodded. "Theater sets. Magic props."

"All of it a shell she designed to surround the real treasure: this place. The place where nothing is fake, and yet a place that, like their relationship, remained hidden from the outside world."

Gabe pulled the journal out of his pocket and we turned to the last page.

"'Heaven,'" he read. "'Where miracles can occur. Where, like the true Queen of the Night, you can rise again.'"

"That's this place, Gabe. I think Charlotte built this as a refuge for Frances when she was sick. A spot where she could surround herself with beauty. With plants from all the places they'd traveled, worked, been together."

He nodded. "But when Frances died, Charlotte covered it all up. Waiting for someone to come along and solve the mystery of the manor."

"But we haven't," I said. "Not yet."

Gabe tapped the fountain. "We need to make this place live again."

"But how?"

CHAPTER 24

THE FOUNTAIN

"You go that way, I'll go this way," Gabe said, pointing back to the greenhouse. "And if you find a ladder or button, don't wait—run back to the door."

We separated and began searching for anything that looked like . . . well, another puzzle. The search did not start well. Just more parched plants and browned leaves—not what I was looking for. I also couldn't shake the image of Hyacinth trapped in the basement, waiting for help. I choked back my worry and my sadness and kept searching.

Turning another corner, I came upon a low iron bench painted green.

It was facing the fountain. Behind it, I recognized birch bark on a dead tree. The bench was too small for two people, which was weird for a park bench. The ones near my house were large enough for at least two people and a gazillion pigeons.

Then I remembered: Frances must have sat in her wheelchair, hoping for a recovery that never came. If Charlotte had built this place for her, maybe she sat on this bench while Frances was next to her in her chair.

For a moment, I was sure I caught the ghostly image of a woman in a wheelchair out of the corner of my eye.

"Gabe!" I called. "I think this is it."

I heard his footsteps hurrying over. I showed him the bench and risked telling him about the ghost.

"They must have sat here together," I said. "Maybe we need to do the same?"

Gabe sat on the bench, and I crouched down where I thought Frances must have parked her chair. Nothing happened. All we could see was the fountain and the dead plants.

"Are we supposed to be looking at something? Like in the map room?" Gabe asked. "We already saw the fountain."

"I don't know." My voice was breaking. I was starting to panic. Time was running out—for everything. Hyacinth might be drowning.

Drowning. Water. Pipes!

"Gabe, you said the plants here didn't have sunlight or water."

"Basic plant necessities."

"We can't do anything about the sunlight, as far as I can tell. But there must be pipes in here, right?"

"A greenhouse this size would definitely have had some kind of irrigation system."

"I think I know how to save Hyacinth. We need to get the water from the basement to here through the pipes."

We narrowed our eyes and looked back up at the ceiling. Sure enough, a series of thin pipes ran along the underside of the girders, ending in hundreds of sprinkler heads.

"I don't see any sign of rust on those," Gabe said. "So they're dry."

"But Hyacinth said they were running water all the time, so why didn't any of it come on in here?"

"It must not be connected," Gabe said. "There has to be some kind of faucet or something that joins up the pipes outside to the system in here."

"A faucet? Really? There's no way it's that simple."

It wasn't.

We sped through the greenhouse, doing our best to follow the pipes on the ceiling like the paths in a maze. We finally traced them back to a single pipe that ran down the back wall and disappeared behind a stand of dead pineapple bushes. We walked behind the bushes and found what we were looking for: a tiled wall covered with dozens of pipes and faucets.

"It looks like a shower stall for an octopus," I said.

"It's a puzzle," Gabe said, tracing the lines of the pipes in the air. "None of them are connected yet. There's a sequence we need to figure out."

"Meaning?"

He ran his fingers along one of the pipes. "See? This one is connected only at one end. If I turned on the water, it would just spray in the air."

"And that doesn't help Hyacinth at all."

"Right. We need to connect them all, and then connect them to the water main."

I looked around everywhere, but I couldn't see any other bits of pipe lying around. "So how do we connect them?"

As we stared at the mess of pipes and faucets, an imaginary analog clock—like the ones in Gabe's kitchen—ticked in my head, the second hand moving around the circle. The other hands moved, too, but more slowly. Rotating, rotating . . .

"I have an idea!" I said. "What if the pipes aren't missing connections—we just need to turn them around to join them up?"

I walked up to the wall and grabbed one section of pipe. It was a bit stuck after a century of disuse, but with a little grunt, I yanked it so that it was now pointing up. That created a connection to the faucet below and the faucet above. There were bolts on the ends of the pipes that I tightened to make the seal waterproof.

I took a step back, smiling. "The faucets stay put and stay off for now. We have to create one single line so that the water comes in from one spot and then goes out to the main pipe."

"A single line made up of dozens of moving parts."

"A beginning and an end."

"You're a genius storyteller AND a plumber," Gabe said.

"You pointed it out." I put a hand on his shoulder. "We really are a great team."

"But we're missing a member. Let's hurry."

We began turning and rotating all the sections of pipe. It was harder than it sounds. Every connection we made had to sync with all the other sections as well.

I turned an L-shaped pipe to meet up with a red metal faucet. I was about to tighten the bolt when Gabe stopped me.

"No, if we lock *that* one in, we can't get water to that yellow faucet down *here*. Which means if we turned it on, the water would start spilling out of the pipe over there." He pointed to the far left, where a long bit of pipe was faucet-less and pointing to the floor.

After a period of trial and error, we finally created a single line. All the faucets could be turned on, and the water would come from a single pipe in the floor and out to the single pipe off the top.

We were just about to turn it on when we heard the squish-squish of wet feet coming down the path behind us.

Gabe began to shake, too scared to turn around.

I wasn't.

The footsteps grew louder, and the soaking wet vision of a girl holding a crowbar emerged from behind a huge pot.

"HYACINTH! You died and came back to haunt us!" I rushed to hug her astral remains.

Hyacinth held up a hand to stop me.

"Still not a ghost," she said.

"And you still have both hands!"

She nodded. "The guillotine *was* a magic trick. There was a false section of the blade that contracted like a telescope when it fell."

Gabe shuddered. "But you had no way of knowing that when you put your arm in."

"That's why it was called the Guillotine of *Trust*," she said. "Still bruised me a bit, though."

Gabe hugged her. "So how did you get out?"

"The water. It put the fires out but kept pouring in. I tore off the top of a crate with the crowbar, then used that like a raft to float up to the door. The crowbar also came in handy with the door—I had to crank that open. But here I am!"

"Well, you're still my favorite ghost," I said, hugging her for real.

She hugged me back and then Gabe joined us. It suddenly felt awesome and warm in the dry greenhouse. Like things were back to the way they should always have been.

"So have you figured it all out?" asked Hyacinth, letting us go and shaking more water out of her shoes.

I stepped aside and pointed to the wall of pipes.

"Would you like to do the honors?"

"Honors?"

"For the first time in a century, life will return to Glyndebourne Manor."

Hyacinth wiped away a tear and stepped forward. She put her hand on the central faucet and turned.

CHAPTER 25

CHARLOTTE AND FRANCES

Nothing happened. At least, not for a few seconds.

"Charlotte does have a flair for the dramatic," I joked.

Then there was a gurgling noise, and the pipes began to shake.

"MORE GHOSTS!" I clapped. But Gabe didn't look scared.

"Not ghosts," he said.

"That's just the water pushing a hundred years of stale air out," Hyacinth explained. "But so far, so good."

The pipes stopped shaking. Then a fine mist began to fall from the ceiling, settling on the dried stubs and lifeless branches.

Gabe lifted his head and laughed as beads of water formed on his cheeks. "Isn't it wonderful?"

"I'm already wet enough, thanks," Hyacinth said.

I closed my eyes and imagined I was a plant soaking up the life-giving water.

Gabe read my mind. "It'll take a while, and some tender loving care, but things will grow here again."

"But don't they also need some sunlight?" I pointed up at the roof.

"I guess that's a job for me and Bertie," Hyacinth said, tapping the crowbar against her palm.

At that moment, the greenhouse rang out with a series of loud clicks and clangs, like someone was unlocking a huge door. A beam of silver light came down from the ceiling, illuminating the fountain, which now sprang to life.

"Wow!" we all said together.

The whole greenhouse vibrated with the squeal of metal hinges as the wooden roof began to lift and separate like petals on a flower. The opening revealed the night sky. It was filled with twinkling stars and the shining silver moon.

"Hello, Halloween moon," I said, expecting to feel a wave of sadness. But I was weirdly . . . happy.

"Maybe this place is the real treasure?" I said to Hyacinth.

"I know as much as you do," she replied. "But that seems about right. Everything here is real. It's beautiful. It's special. And the only way to find it was to look at things the right way."

"Seeing Frances and Charlotte's life together," Gabe said.

"A little money might have been nice, just to cover your reward for solving this."

I took a deep breath. "We all solved this together. We don't need the reward money. You tell Charlotte and Frances's story. That's reward enough for us."

Hyacinth hugged me.

"I guess a small wedding isn't so bad," Gabe said.

"I think I know the perfect venue." I smiled and then turned to Hyacinth. "There's one more place we should show you. I think it meant a lot to Charlotte and Frances."

Gabe and I led her to the bench, but I stopped in my tracks as I spied something resting on the painted iron. It wasn't there before.

"Hyacinth, did you see this bench already?"

"No. I sloshed my way straight to you guys."

I was shaking now. "Gabe, did you leave the journal on the seat?"

"Nope. I've got it right here in my pants."

"Then how do you explain that?" I pointed at a sheet of yellowed notepaper lying on the bench. A few dried birch leaves had come to rest on top.

"I—I can't."

I reached over and carefully brushed aside the leaves. It was a letter. I began reading but quickly stopped.

I passed the letter to Hyacinth. "I think Charlotte and Frances's great-grandniece should be the one to read this."

And so she did.

CHAPTER 26

THE BIRCH TREE

March 3, 1911

It happened yesterday morning. Spent the day making preparations. The weather has been warm the past few days, as if winter is holding its breath, giving us a break. I'm glad I was by her side. She was resting for a small time in the conservatory. She loved it there. Two weeks ago, I set up a bed near the fountain so she could sleep under the glass roof, the stars shining on her. The last night, we were resting together on the cot, her head on my shoulder. She tried to whisper to me, but she was in too much pain to speak at first. I told her it was all right. I hummed the short little song I'd composed for her after buying that ridiculous pianola. She managed to tap her finger on my collarbone to the rhythm. Then she looked at me. Her eyes were clear, the first time in a long time.

"It will happen soon," she said.

"It doesn't matter," I replied, sighing.

She tapped on my shoulder once more, this time urgently.

"It will happen. You need to be ready."

I looked at her. "We don't need to talk about this now. Just rest."

She pressed her finger into my shoulder. She closed her eyes, breathed in as deeply as she could and said, "What will you do when I'm no longer here?"

We'd discussed this so many times. I repeated what I knew she wanted me to say. "I'll plant a birch tree here in the earth, and you shall lie below. And you'll grow so tall you'll reach over the house. The birds will nest, and they will sing to you in the spring and summer. When they fly away and your branches are bare, I will play for you and try my best to sing. And you will never be lonely."

She shook her head slightly. "No, I meant what will you do?"

I couldn't tell her what I'd been planning, the idea that had appeared in my mind when she'd become sick again and we realized there was no getting better. That while she was too ill to leave the greenhouse, I was hard at work on a new plan for the house. I couldn't tell her that what I would do was be haunted by her forever. That I knew she wouldn't truly be gone, and that I'd search for her after death. That the house, now in its final stages, would be a mausoleum. I closed my eyes and listened to *her irregular breathing. My last words to her were a lie.*

"I'll keep working. Travel around the world, enchant yet more audiences with our sets and technical tricks."

She sighed contentedly. "Exactly."

I cradled her in my arms, and soon, we were both asleep—me for a few fitful hours, and her forever.

Tomorrow, I will begin the process of closing off the conservatory. Even thinking of it makes me sick. Xavier, the whole brood—they can never know what secrets lie within the walls of this house. They'd use it against me. They wouldn't understand that she was my wife, now and forever. The house will continue on, as it always does, but at its heart will lie a secret, the secret of our love.

CHAPTER 27

THE BRIDESMATE OF FRANKENSTEIN'S SISTER

"Zed, if you don't take those fangs out *right now*—" Sam glared at me so hard, it felt like a virtual wooden dagger aimed at my bloodless heart.

We were back at Glyndebourne Manor for the wedding of the century! The greenhouse, to be precise, which Jo and Sam had agreed was the perfect place to tie the knot. Even though it was now December, the greenhouse was still nice and warm.

"Drats!" I said. My effort to sneak a little vampire style into the wedding had been discovered.

Gabe chuckled. "Foiled again, Count Dracula!"

I took out the fangs and smiled for the camera. I choked up a bit as Sam and Jo held hands and kissed.

Sure, it would have been a better picture if we'd all had bat wings and cloaks, but it still came out pretty good.

231

We had gathered together in the middle of the green-house. Sam and Jo had won the "small wedding" argument. The fact that there wasn't any real treasure—at least not a monetary one—helped swing things to their side.

So it was the Lindens, the Watsons (which, TBH, pushed the limits of the definition of "small"), some friends of Sam and Jo's from here and school, and of course, Hyacinth and Bertie.

The celebrant performed the ceremony dressed in Charlotte's costume for *Aida*. The headdress alone almost reached the ceiling.

"They make a lovely couple, don't they?" said Leslie, Jo's awesome uncle, as we sat together near the birch tree. Gabe and Bertie had transplanted a young birch sapling from the grounds of Glyndebourne. And Jimi had helped build a new bigger bench next to the original for the special spot. Enough room for me, Aloysius and Leslie.

The buffet was set up a few feet away, and almost every-one else was hanging out there.

"Aloysius agrees with you," I said to him. "So do Charlotte and Frances. I can feel it."

Leslie reached over and gave Aloysius a pat on the head. "The dead need to be honored, always," he said.

"Does that explain the floral arrangements too?" Gabe asked, walking over with a plate piled high.

Leslie chuckled. "You know that I hate to see anything go to waste."

The arrangements were all made from dead branches and flowers found around the greenhouse gardens. But like everything Leslie touched, they had a dignity and beauty.

I downed another cookie—this one shaped like a cookie punching another cookie.

"Jo insisted on the design," Jennie laughed, putting a fresh plate of them down on the buffet table.

"Well, it looks and tastes amazing. All the food does!"

Jennie bowed. "Thank you, Zed. Oh! The samosas are almost all gone." She hurried off to the kitchen for more.

Jo came over, holding a bouquet of birch branches and dried-out roses. "Zed, this place is absolutely perfect."

"I think Charlotte and Frances would have been honored to host your wedding here."

"Not that. I mean, that *is* amazing, but I'm talking about the other stuff. Bertie says Jimi and I can come by after my honeymoon to rummage through the manor. I can't wait to see how all this amazing stuff works."

"Respect the ghosts, though," Gabe said. "They are ruthless."

Jimi walked over, his plate piled high with fry bread. "The floating ghost was probably done with mirrors and lights. And the picture falling and stuff? Had to be some kind of mechanical device that did that."

"Or the ghost Zed saw in the window did it," Jo said.

Jimi shook his head. "Nah, that was probably Hyacinth dancing in her closet."

Hyacinth looked up from the buffet. "That wasn't me. I was making up the beds."

"Then who . . . ?" Gabe's voice trailed off.

A slight breeze rustled the leaves of the birch tree. We smiled at each other.

"It's too bad you kids had to miss Halloween trick-or-treating," Leslie said. "Even if it was for a good cause."

"Funny story about that," I said. "Right after we solved the mystery of the manor, we went—"

But before I could finish, the DJ called out, "Yo! Time for the FIRST DANCE!"

Rap music began pumping out of a speaker by the fountain.

Sam came over and put an arm around Jo's waist. "They're playing our song," she said. They kissed and then spun away to the dance floor.

Leslie got up and shook out his legs. "You got time to explain your funny story as we start grooving?"

"Later. I promise."

He nodded, then shimmied over to the dance floor.

I filled my pockets with more cookies and got ready to join them. I'd requested the *Munsters* theme, the Charleston and the latest Carly Rae bangers, so my feet were already tingling.

But something made me stop for a second, like an invisible hand on my shoulder.

It was Hyacinth's hand on my shoulder.

"You can feel it too, right?" she asked.

I nodded. "Charlotte and Frances are at peace."

"And I think they're here right now. Bertie and I plan to open this place as a museum. Some ticket sales might help keep it alive."

"That's a pretty good treasure."

We fist-bumped, and I let my fingers stay a moment longer than necessary.

"I'm still not a ghost, Zed."

"Rats."

We made our way over to the dance floor, where Gabe

was doing the Charleston with my mom. At one point, she lifted him up and he glanced into the bowl of the fountain.

His eyes went as big as Jennie's mushroom quiche. "YOU HAVE GOT TO BE KIDDING ME!" he yelled.

"Are you okay?" My mom quickly lowered him back down.

But Gabe was doubled over with laughter.

The DJ paused the tunes, and we all gathered around.

"Please tell me there's a ghost haunting the fountain," I pleaded.

He shook his head. "No. *Look*."

I pulled up a couple of chairs, and Hyacinth and I peered over the lip of the fountain. It had now been running continuously for weeks. The constant stream of water had revealed one last secret.

That ornately decorated mosaic inside the fountain wasn't made of tiles at all. The paste "jewels" and paint had almost completely washed away, revealing an entire bowl made of gold bricks.

"Wow!" said Hyacinth in an awed whisper. "That should help cover some of the repairs."

I looked back over my shoulder at Sam and Jo. "I know you wanted the wedding small, but any chance you'd like a slightly more elaborate honeymoon?"

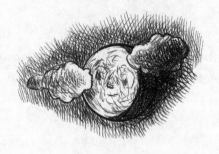

THE STORY I TOLD LESLIE
(AFTER WE'D FINISHED GROOVING)

I shivered as the sun set and an eerie cool mist settled in around the nearby houses. The house I stood before was barely visible in the gloom.

I walked up the rickety front stairs, paused for a second and rang the doorbell.

"Mrs. Gianelli? Are you there?"

I waited, holding my breath. No answer. I frowned. Then I rang the doorbell again. A cat hissed in the distance. Still no answer.

I turned to my green-hued companion and spoke clearly despite my long sharp fangs. "You try."

Gabe, his costume now tailored to fit, pressed the button.

Finally, the door slowly opened a crack, and Mrs. Gianelli's face appeared in the sliver of light. She was wearing an apron and holding a large knife!

"AHHHH!" Gabe screamed.

I reached out and grabbed his arm to stop him from bolting. "Trick or treat!" I said.

"Um, it's November 2." Mrs. Gianelli closed the door slightly.

My mouth quivered.

She threw the door wide open. "Just kidding, Zed. Happy Follow-Halloween!"

Yes, my awesome neighbors had heard about the tragedy of the missed holiday—in an interview we'd done about solving yet another mystery—and had decided to extend the festivities.

"What's a few extra days of running the fog machine and letting the squirrels eat my pumpkins?" said Mrs. Gianelli.

I take back all the mean stuff I said earlier about adults and holidays.

Well, some of it, anyway. Mr. Ohi had turned off his lights and refused to answer the door. He had also posted a letter on his porch protesting his one-pumpkin rating and left a bag of (blech) candy corn.

"Mrs. Gianelli, you are the best!"

She tossed at least five full-size Coffee Crisps into my bag, then slipped a CD of Pavarotti favorites into Gabe's.

"Nothing for the ghost?" I said. I stepped aside, revealing

Hyacinth—dressed in a silvery flapper dress and holding a birchbark-patterned bag.

Mrs. Gianelli started. "Oh! I didn't see you there."

"That's how we ghosts roll," said Hyacinth with a smile.

Mrs. Gianelli put some Kit Kats into her bag. "Can I ask why this ghost is carrying a crowbar?"

Gabe chuckled. "It's kind of an inside joke."

We headed back out into the mist.

"Thanks again, Mrs. Gianelli," I called back over my shoulder with a tear in my eye. "Happy Follow-Halloween!"

ACKNOWLEDGMENTS

BASIL: This book couldn't have happened without the incredible response to *The Fabulous Zed Watson!*, so thank you all for reading, reviewing and buying the book, nominating us for awards, and sending along messages from yourselves, your kids, your students and your families—it's been an amazing experience so far!

Night of the Living Zed was made possible by our superstar editor Yash and the rest of the amazing crew at HarperCollins. Thank you for believing that Zed and Gabe should return for another adventure!

More special thanks: Larry Switzky, for the help researching and the fun conversations about turn-of-the-century stagecraft!

Shout-out to the wombats for assisting with silly names and places and fun little jokes, and a special shout-out to

Molly Sayles for musical suggestions. I managed to include Shostakovich! Truly legendary.

I'd also like to thank the people who make me who I am today: the Carlins and the Sylvesters; Élie, Kaeli, Paul, Roz, Casey, Amelia, Eoin. And the three couples who made sure beautiful, wonderful weddings were firmly on my mind while I wrote: Justin and Lindsay, Sasha and Geena, and my sister, Erin, and her (now our) David. Thank you to Gimli the dog for the cuddles—they were instrumental in finishing this book.

I read a lot of literary love letters while preparing to write this book, and Charlotte and Frances owe a debt of gratitude to the letters of Vita Sackville-West and Virginia Woolf, Edith Wharton, Ken Kesey, Emily Dickinson and Susan Gilbert, Christopher Isherwood, and many other literary greats and queer pioneers for putting their stories down on paper long before I ever picked up a pen.

Finally, thank you always to my co-writer and dad, Kevin Sylvester. These books would not be fun at all without you. Thank you for letting me put some more Russian opera in this one—payback for all the Wagner, ha!

KEVIN: I echo everything Basil has said and add a few more thanks of my own. Above all, to my amazing wife, Laura Carlin, for everything.

The support for Zed's first adventure was overwhelming.

Thanks to all the booksellers and book readers and book award judges who embraced Zed and shared their story. Too many to name them all (which is a lovely thought), but special thanks to Jeffrey Canton, Shelagh Rogers (enjoy "retirement!"), the DiTerlizzis, the gang at High Five Books, E. Train, Kenneth Oppel, Robin Stevenson, Rob Bittner, Alex Gino, S. Bear Bergman . . . I mean, too many to name.

I am gobsmacked.